SUSPENSION

⚬

- Between Two Realms -

Stella McMillan

SUSPENSION – Between Two Realms – Stella McMillan
Copyright © 2013, B J BREE

Publisher: B J BREE
Brisbane, Australia

www.stellamcmillan.com.au

ISBN: 0957881339
ISBN 13: 9780957881334

National Library of Australia, Canberra, ACT

Cataloguing-in-publication data:

   1. Literature & Fiction   2. Metaphysical/Past Lives/New Age

Consciousness

To those of a *limited consciousness*, Earth is here to be exploited by them. Her riches are there for the taking.

To those of an *expanded consciousness*, Earth is here to be protected by them. Her riches are there to be held in trust for future generations.

To those of an *enlightened consciousness*, Earth is a precious treasure – there for all to behold. Her beauty is a source of joy and wonder.

Only those of an *enlightened consciousness* can view Gaia, the Mother:

From The Rim

Contents

For Lisa Ann, Mark and Laurie

Dedication

This book is dedicated to those who are true seekers of Light, this being enlightenment and understanding of a spiritual nature. May its contents bring another perspective to all who are devoted to the protection of Mother Earth and who are inspired by an ardent desire to bring enlightenment to all who reside here.

Acknowledgements

I offer my gratitude to my family and my loyal friends who have supported and assisted me through this long writing and publishing process spanning many years.

Special thanks for their gentle advice and continued encouragement during the writing of this series of books must go to Patricia, Rosalind, Kay and Corinne.

Appreciation is expressed to Andy for his technical expertise. I thank Joseph for his support where my books are concerned and who, along with Annie, made the trek up the mountain, so that I could bring the swaying suspension bridge to life for the front cover of this book, *SUSPENSION – Between Two Realms –*

Foreword

SUSPENSION – Between Two Realms –

This book is a companion to the **Stella McMillan** six-book fiction Series, which has been published in the form of two trilogies. As such, it can be enjoyed alone, or read in conjunction with the other books of this Series.

The purpose of **SUSPENSION – Between Two Realms –** is to release the set of Discourses that was presented to Paula during and after her many sojourns into the spiritual realm of the Astral plane where she met with her Spirit Guide, Gerard, on numerous occasions. Paula's visits there were interspersed with her time-travelling exploits and experiences, which seemed very real to her at the time. These challenging and life-changing experiences were described within the pages of the last two books of the second Trilogy, these books being **ERROR PROFOUND** and **ERA of DISCERNMENT.**

First Trilogy: *ERA/ERROR of UNDERSTANDING*

ERROR of UNDERSTANDING found Paula viewing scenes that were familiar to her as these played themselves out in *Victorian Victoria,* in Australia, commencing in 1867. Mesmerised by the drama that was unfolding between Charles Lyndhurst and his young wife, Louisa, while his mistress, Sylvia, watched her world disintegrating around her, Paula receded to a place deep within herself. She forgot all about the physical life that she was leading in Los Angeles just prior to the commencement of the new twenty-first century.

She followed the lives of Louisa and Charles as they attended the various events that were arranged to welcome His Royal Highness, Prince Alfred, Duke of Edinburgh, to the Australian colonies on the first Royal Tour of that country in 1867. Louisa's attraction to the young Phillip Carstairs stirred deep emotions within Paula who watched from afar. Charles' deep love for his Sylvia consumed him during the first few months of this arranged marriage, which neither party wanted. Their interests lay elsewhere.

ERROR PERPETUATED continued the drama as Charles continued his liaison with Sylvia while, at the same time, he demanded that Louisa follow his stern and strict directives at all times. Louisa, being just as determined to flout his authority over her, fought him every step of the way. Their battles were many and always the spectre of Phillip stood between them. Louisa's love for Phillip electrified and frightened her at the same time. Her illicit meetings with him were a constant source of excitement for her in the life that she viewed as being staid, stodgy, suffocating and soul-destroying.

Lady Elizabeth Lyndhurst was concerned that her son, Charles, would not realise the precious diamond that had been placed into his hands on the day of his marriage to Louisa. When he did, it was almost too late to retrieve the situation.

The emotional roller-coaster ride, on which Paula had embarked while delving into this ongoing nineteenth century drama, was resonating with her as she fought for life in a hospital setting during the final few months of the twentieth century while being far removed, in a physical sense, from Victorian Melbourne.

ERA of UNDERSTANDING brought new challenges to the fore as the lives of Louisa, Charles, Sylvia, Phillip and Elizabeth were played out to their ultimate conclusion. This occurred long before the last days of the nineteenth century had been extinguished. That they were replaying old scenes from a previous Scottish lifetime was unknown to them – at a conscious level – at the time. Paula was but the silent witness.

Second Trilogy: *ERA/ERROR of DISCERNMENT*

AWAKENING TO AWARENESS found Paula reviewing her early life in a casino in Las Vegas while she was drifting in an out-of-body reality. Her involvement with Lachlan Jefferson happened then as she sought to rescue her younger sister from a situation, from which the young girl did not wish to be rescued. While assisting Lachlan to trap an individual who was a renowned confidence trickster, she fell in love with him while he was married to someone else. Their adventures while attempting to defeat the slick, suave Lucas, brought great triumph, as well as danger and death.

From the detached reality of her hospital setting, Paula reviewed this earlier period of her current life until a definite and life-altering decision was forced upon her.

With the introduction to her Spirit Guide, Gerard, came another set of circumstances, with which Paula was required to grapple while she refused to accept that she had been the young Louisa in a previous time. In his reality of the Astral realm, Gerard counselled Paula wisely as she struggled with the finality of this decision of gigantic proportions – from her perspective.

ERROR PROFOUND brought Paula back to the world of the physical although her contact with Gerard continued and this remained strong. He guided her to his reality at the Astral level where many of their in-depth conversations took place. She visited a massive dome structure, which was perched on the banks of a lake. She took a canoe ride with him and, while seated in a cave behind a magical and mighty waterfall, she listened to his words of wisdom. He showed her a place of healing inside the glass dome, as well as another one that was within the walls of a white lighthouse.

At the same time, Paula was attempting to remain grounded in her *real world* with her husband as she tried to coax him to relocate, with their young son, to a desert oasis outside the city of Las Vegas as the first two years of the twenty-first century began to unfold.

With Gerard, she accepted the challenge to record a set of Discourses on spiritual enlightenment and understanding. What she was to do with this ever-growing collection of writings, she did not know. These had come to her in the early hours of the morning after her regular attendances at her spiritual meditation group. She was pondering on these matters when the Twin Towers were destroyed and life on Earth changed forever.

ERA of DISCERNMENT brought about a new set of circumstances as Paula struggled to understand the concept of death and the consequences of errors made in one life coming to the fore to be faced in the next life, or in a subsequent one. Searching for answers to spiritual issues such as these, she regressed voluntarily to another lifetime. This time, it was to Scotland around the time of Bonnie Prince Charlie and the futile battle surrounding his attempt to secure his lost crown.

Once again, not only was it the familiarity of the scenes, which were taking place, that was haunting Paula, but also, it was the fact that she recognised the people who were around her back then, in that time-frame. They were, also, the same people whom she recognised as being in Victorian Victoria in the country that became known as Australia. Charles was there, as was Sylvia and Phillip. They were with her back in both of those lifetimes, albeit with different physical bodies and different identities, but with the same personalities and similar attitudes to life. Paula knew, without any doubt whatsoever, that she had lived previously with these same people. She had loved them then, as she loved them now.

Finally, the set of Discourses that Gerard was releasing to her began to make more sense. There was one fact, of which she was absolutely certain. She was no longer the same person that she had been before her physical body was wheeled into the hospital operating theatre on the Gold Coast in Australia on 10 September, 1999.

What a fateful day that had been for Paula, as well as being the day of her thirty-fifth birthday – in this current life experience on the planet known as Earth.

ى‑ص

Consciousness

To those of a *limited consciousness*, Earth is here to be
exploited by them. Her riches are there for the taking.

To those of an *expanded consciousness*, Earth is here to be protected by
them. Her riches are there to be held in trust for future generations.

To those of an *enlightened consciousness*, Earth is a precious treasure –
there for all to behold. Her beauty is a source of joy and wonder.

Only those of an *enlightened consciousness* can view Gaia, the Mother:

From The Rim

From The Rim
From the Rim of Earth, I view her beneath me

The canopy of the night sky enfolds me.
The darkness of Earth troubles me.
Her oceans, her landmass, struggle to breathe.
She trembles; she quivers – longs to be free.

From the rim of Earth, I view feather-fingers.
These creep imperceptibly; their promise lingers.
Dawn spreads slowly over land and sea.
There is great promise. *Light* is all I see.

From the rim of Earth, I view an horizon of Light.
Love follows, on angels' wings, Divine Light.
Light cleanses. Love heals anew. So bright!
A new dawn is here – a wondrous sight.

From the rim of Earth, I view a new era of Love.
The vision so clear, viewed from above.
The darkness shatters and dissipates fast.
Humanity awakens joyfully at last.

From the rim of Earth, I know of a future bright.
I See; I Feel; I Know; I witness Light.
Love Everlasting, peace on Earth, goodwill all.
Divine Will, Divine Light, Divine Love re-born.

From the rim of Earth, I know hope rising;
Hatred, violence, retarded consciousness subsiding.
Love conquers all. Abandon old ways dividing.
As One, strangers embrace in Love unbridled.

From The Rim
From the Rim of Earth, I view her beneath me

From the rim of Earth, I view The Mother in fear.
She quakes; she quivers; the rock a-near.
With one, mighty shudder, she succumbs to fate.
Her children notice her plight too late.

From the rim of Earth, I view panic arise.
All running in panic, nowhere to hide
In God's Love, all could easily abide.
Fear is dominant emotion to rise.

When fire is quelled, damage reviewed.
Earth now populated by so very few.
The Mother now shattered and drained.
Her energy abated; her distress restrained.

"Where to from here?" all ask again.
"Help The Mother heal," comes the refrain.
"How?" is the question; "gently" comes reply
as the sun beats down from a clear sky.

Temperature rising; water so scarce;
food disappearing fast; animals scared.
Hope on horizon; rain appears from nowhere.
Crops peep from rejuvenated Earth.

As God takes away, God gives aplenty.
To ones who survive, appears great bounty.
Blessings are counted by those on surface.
Miracles recounted as life has purpose.

From The Rim
From the Rim of Earth, I view her beneath me

Purpose of life on Earth comes into question
by ones who possess a mind probing reason.
Reason is simple; world out-of-balance;
ones remaining rise to the challenge.

Earth on the mend; Mother smiling again;
her children toil in ways of times olden.
Happiness reigns. Hope springs eternally.
Father Sky, Mother Earth joined fourth-dimensionally.

All are One. Oneness resumed with above.
All toil together in Universal Love.
All play together in unbroken bond.
All pray together, bound by universal code.

Divine Intervention a necessary sequence
when children run rampant, denying consequence.
Unfortunate, but true, when Light, Love denied;
to Buddha/Christ Light, most were blind.

All clear; all cleansed; all healed presently.
The Mother shining so brightly in galaxy;
her rightful place resumed in heavenly sky.
Her vibratory frequency currently sky high.

From third to fourth dimension a quantum leap –
her population fought to keep her deep
in the quagmire of third dimensional life.
Her courage, in rising so fast, brought strife.

From The Rim
From the Rim of Earth, I view her beneath me

With turmoil behind her, Mother seeks to heal.
Her children shaken, saddened by experience real.
Many loved ones missing; didn't answer 'the call'.
Believed life could go on with no change at all.

Impossible feat to accomplish for most –
rising to fourth dimension a cause lost.
Those steeped in denial of Creator-of-All
were first to experience gigantic fall.

Wailing, weeping, as earthly return denied.
Understanding reason impossible for ones blind.
Blind to True Reality by own choice.
All others, in God's Great Love, rejoice!

Stella McMillan
10 October, 2012

Part One

Prologue

Paula and Lachlan's life was filled to overflowing with an incredibly-deep love when the birth of their second daughter, Sophia, occurred. Sophia was born on 19 March, 2002. At the time, Lachlan was determined to persuade a reluctant Paula to return to Los Angeles with him and their young family one year on from that date. Paula was just as determined to remain in their desert hideaway.

Their son, Byron, was born at the end of 1990 and around the time of the first Gulf War, which lasted for five months. Twelve months on from Sophia's birth, the second Gulf War commenced. On both occasions, Iraq was invaded by coalition forces.

The likelihood of Lachlan being successful in persuading Paula to return to his old home in Los Angeles on 19 March, 2003, was not high; nor was this event a foregone conclusion. She would have been alarmed by world events that were overtaking them at that time and she would have elected, in all probability, to remain in their safe and secluded home on the outskirts of Las Vegas.

World events do have a habit of intervening to alter the pre-planned life-paths of many who incarnate here. This is an inevitable fact-of-life on Earth, unfortunately.

So, what has the *Stella McMillan* Series been outlining? Were these writings simply romantic fiction? Or, was there, perhaps, a deeper, underlying theme? We can explore this question in Part One of this book while Part Two will be devoted to the long-promised Discourses. For now, let us return to Paula and Lachlan to see where life has taken them.

Chapter One

10 September, 2012

Paula awoke suddenly from a deep sleep. Her eyes opened instantly. Coming to the realisation that she was in her bed, with Lachlan beside her, she wondered momentarily what had roused her from the deep sleep that she had been enjoying.

She kissed Lachlan. He did not stir. Their bedroom was in semi-darkness. Leaving the bed, she went immediately to check on her sleeping children, although Byron was no longer living at home with them on a permanent basis. He spent his time between the Los Angeles home where his studies kept him busy and his parents' home in Las Vegas. Melissa and Sophia were sleeping peacefully in their respective bedrooms.

With coffee cup in hand, Paula made her way to her meditation room where she knew that she would not be disturbed. She moved to open the drapes on the windows, thereby revealing sweeping views of the Mojave Desert. Dawn was breaking. How she loved this time of morning, just as she loved their secluded home on the outskirts of the city. Fervently, she hoped that the city would never creep closer, thus invading their space and their special place.

To this day, Lachlan referred to their home, which Paula had designed in the shape of a figure-eight, as their spacecraft in the desert. To Paula, the shape represented something else. To her, the figure-eight when flipped on its side was simply the sign of Infinity. On this issue, as well as on the issue of their return to the Los Angeles home of Lachlan's childhood, they had agreed to disagree.

Cradling the cup in her two hands, she was held spellbound by the spectacular colours of the sky as night turned slowly to day. With a deep sigh, she slid into her meditation chair that was positioned by the window and which gave her an uninterrupted view of her precious desert where she could watch the ongoing display of dawn's daily magic being played out before her eyes.

Placing the cup on the table beside her, she closed her eyes momentarily. Almost instantly, she was in another place. Paula found that she was standing at the end of a long suspension bridge. This bridge traversed a deep ravine that had tall trees growing on both embankments. At the end of the bridge, there was a coffee shop. It was more of a meeting place than a coffee shop in reality.

Paula gave a soft laugh while asking herself the question regarding which reality. Once across the other side, she would be in the *reality* of the Astral plane where her Spirit Guide, Gerard, would be waiting for her. The sudden urge to cross the bridge swept over her. There was time still. Her family would sleep for few hours yet.

Paula walked quickly across the bridge.

She followed the path to the area at the rear of the coffee shop where she located him. He was wearing a long, white robe and his dark hair was flopping over his forehead. He was sitting alone on the two-person swing, with its multi-coloured awning flapping in the slight breeze. He smiled at her as she approached. Definitely, it was Lachlan's smile of welcome, laced with love.

She positioned herself on the swing beside him. She knew that Gerard had been waiting there for her.

"Good morning, sweet one," Gerard greeted her.

Paula glanced across to the magnificent dome in the distance as the early rays of the morning sun glistened on its glass exterior. She smiled up at Gerard.

"Good morning! It is dawn here, also," she commented. "I didn't plan on coming here today."

"Are you certain about that?" he asked, with a laugh.

"No, I guess not, as I'm not certain about anything anymore . . . well, not since I met you anyway!"

"There's never been a time when you did not know me," Gerard corrected her.

Silence engulfed them. Eventually, it was Paula who broke the reverie that was enveloping them.

"Gerard, I need you to clarify something for me."

"If it is within my power to do so, I will assist you. What is your question?"

"There is much hype in my world regarding the possibility of the end of the world happening before 2012 has concluded. Is this likely?"

Gerard gave a deep sigh before responding to her question. His words came softly into her mind.

"The theory is based on a calendar that was compiled by individuals who belonged to a certain race of people that inhabited Earth long ago. These men were extremely advanced astronomers and their calendar was based on the position of the stars in the night sky. They knew the date of any day in any year by the position of those stars at any given moment. Their calendar was compiled to the end of 2012. Why a conclusion such as that would be drawn from the fact of the calendar's ending is inexplicable. Does this answer your question?"

"I guess so, but it's stated that the stars in the night sky will change their positions after this current year has concluded," Paula persisted with her questioning.

"Stated by whom?" Gerard queried. "There are factors that could cause such an event to occur. One such occurrence could be that an asteroid might give the planet a glancing blow as it is passing by. There could be a series of volcanic eruptions happening simultaneously around the world and this could alter slightly the planet's orbit. Man could cause Earth to move her position if he were to be so unwise as to cause a series of nuclear explosions in order to cause harm to a perceived enemy. A *Doctor Strangelove* could appear to alter, in a negative manner, humanity's pre-planned pathway to spiritual enlightenment. Anything is possible when a great imbalance occurs. The inhabitants of your planet have caused a great imbalance now as the wants of the individual outweigh the needs of the whole. The physical life has become more important than the spiritual life. Do you not witness this in everyday life?"

"You are probably right, Gerard. Everything seems to be out-of-control in many countries. No one appears to have any answers to all of these extremely negative events that are happening. These are flashing at us every night on our TV news broadcasts," Paula replied, before asking tentatively her next question. "I was wondering if you considered that the time is right now to release those Discourses that you gave to me?"

"The timing of their release is in your hands. Follow your own inner guidance on the matter, as your God-given in-built directional compass will never guide you astray. Listen closely and you will know the exact moment when it is wise to release them. There will be few who will pay much heed to them, in all probability. However, it will not be possible for anyone to return to us on the Astral plane, after his or her current Earth experience has concluded, while complaining that no warnings were given. Does this answer your question?"

"I suppose it does," Paula conceded. "Before I return to my other life today, would it be possible for us to spend a little time together in the special, wondrous place that you refer to as the *New Jerusalem*?"

Standing immediately, Gerard reached for her hand.

As they walked, he placed his arm through Paula's arm. Together and in silence, they took the pathway that led to the island, on which stood this magnificent and massive structure where she had visited with Gerard previously. He leaned closer to her.

"How is it that this same thought entered into our minds simultaneously, do you think?"

In reply, Paula gave a soft laugh as they approached the small, timber bridge that led to the island where the building stood in all its spectacular glory.

It was some time later that Paula opened her eyes while staring out through the windows at the sight of the desert stretched before her. The sun had risen higher in the sky. The coffee beside her was cold. She gave a deep sigh as her consciousness returned to her real world.

Lachlan's voice was emanating from another part of their home as were the shrieks of laughter coming from their two daughters whom they both adored. To Paula, the sound was heaven-sent. Thank God that she had chosen to return when given the definite choice while her physical body was stretched out in an unconscious state on the operating table in the Gold Coast Hospital in Australia all those years ago. It had been fighting for life following a fatal car accident while Paula was floating in another space entirely, with Gerard at her side.

Life had taken her on a very different path from that moment onwards. Her old life in Los Angeles with Lachlan and Byron, prior to that time, resembled an immediate past-life experience to her now. Her entire perspective on life had changed in the instant when she left her physical body on the day of her thirty-fifth birthday. Paula knew, without doubt, that she could never become that person again, no matter how much she tried to revert to the old Paula. Life had moved on. The world around her had moved on. There would never be a time when she could reverse the situation. Finally, Lachlan had come to the acceptance of this fact of life. Thankfully, he had embraced the *new* Paula – warts and all!

However, there had been many moments during the past decade when Paula felt that Lachlan was turning from her, due to her new way of life. Fortunately, they had weathered all storms together.

The accident had occurred in 1999 on her birthday. Today, she was turning forty-eight years of age, so she was entering her forty-ninth year technically. Therefore, she had negotiated successfully seven periods of seven years. Momentarily, she wondered how many other seven-year cycles were available to her in this current embodiment. In the overall scheme of life, this did not matter. The other realm where she visited often was awaiting her arrival, once her physical form was needed by her no longer. But, for today, life was awaiting her here, in this realm. Paula rose slowly from the recliner chair. Her family was waiting for her.

She entered the dining room to the greatest surprise of all. Her twenty-one year old son, Byron, was waiting there. He embraced her warmly. He was eleven years old when Sophia was born to them. Melissa rushed into Paula's outstretched arms then, just as Sophia thrust a gift-wrapped parcel into her mother's hands.

In this flurry of excitement, Paula was caught in the arms of her children.

In an instant, there was a flash-back in time for her. She had been twenty-four years of age when her life collided with Lachlan's world. She was living in Las Vegas back then, also, where she had been enjoying her wild, chaotic lifestyle. She was working in an out-of-the-way, smaller casino where she operated a blackjack table. Almost a quarter-of-a-century had flown by in-a-blink since the first fiery encounter between the two of them. What an amazing journey, she mused.

Suddenly and spontaneously, Lachlan burst into song. As Charles Lyndhurst had sung the birthday song with gusto, at the grand and elaborate celebrations to mark the birthday of his daughter, Mary, in Victorian Melbourne over a century earlier, Lachlan sang *Happy Birthday* to Paula now.

Enthusiastically, their children joined him, thus causing an immediate emotional response within Paula.

As their loud and impromptu rendition ended in cheering and clapping, Paula's spontaneous laughter swept the room. It began as a gurgle that commenced within the depths of her being. It rumbled from her as it burst forth, filling the room with its melodious notes that swirled around them while holding them captive within the tight grip of her deep love for all of them.

And, her family laughed with her.

Glancing across the room to her husband, she smiled at him. She whispered a silent thank-you to Lachlan for his attentiveness and for preparing this surprise birthday breakfast for her.

The love that was visible on Lachlan's face as he gazed back at her was the only gift that Paula needed to make today complete.

Then, he smiled at her. It was a familiar smile that was laced with love.

The smile was Gerard's smile!

Chapter Two

After breakfast, Paula adjourned to the shower. Lachlan had driven the girls to school en route to his office. Byron, who had spent over a decade of his life in Las Vegas, had many friends in the city and he had borrowed Paula's car so that he could visit several of them. Paula was left to her own devices then. She had received strict instructions from Lachlan to be ready when he returned to take her to her birthday lunch. This was a long-standing arrangement that began after the accident when she was on her way to meet him on that other fateful day.

She returned to her meditation room. She had time to spare before his return. Recalling her time spent with Gerard earlier in the morning, she reached for the folder containing the sheets of paper where she had typed the Discourses. These, she had hand-written originally before transferring them carefully to her laptop computer.

Opening the folder, she began to read the first one, which was on the subject of the power of crystals. She was mid-way through reading the large number of pages that the folder contained when the door opened. She glanced up to see Lachlan standing in the doorway.

"Well, fancy finding you in here . . . of all places!" he exclaimed, with eyebrows raised and a somewhat supercilious expression on his face.

"I'm ready and waiting. You're late and I'm filling in time," Paula responded a little defensively, as she rose from the chair. "I'm certain it's not necessary for you to keep up this ritual of collecting me to escort me to my birthday lunch year after year. I could've met you at the restaurant as I'm quite capable of driving myself to the city."

"I've told you. I'll be doing so for the next fifty years."

Paula laughed as he came to her and kissed her.

"You say that every year," she reminded him.

He elaborated on his reason for doing so.

"Otherwise, I'd never be certain of you arriving there. You left me waiting once before . . . remember? Besides, you don't have a car today."

"Oh! So, there's a conspiracy afoot here."

"You'd better believe it!" he replied, as he placed an arm around her shoulder.

Lachlan reached for her while intending to lead her from the room. Paula closed the folder containing the Discourses. She would finish reading them later, she promised herself.

They made a detour, at Lachlan's suggestion, and called at his office in the city. It was an apartment, which had been their temporary home once while they had waited for their secluded, desert home to be constructed. His main office was located in Los Angeles and this smaller one was where he worked when in Las Vegas. His cousin, Stephen, whom Lachlan employed, was there and he greeted Paula warmly while offering birthday greetings to her. Besides being Lachlan's cousin, Stephen was married to Carla, Paula's sister.

After leaving the office, they walked hand-in-hand along the street as they headed towards the restaurant. Suddenly, Lachlan pulled her in a different direction.

"I want to show you something."

They came to a standstill a few blocks away and outside the front of the old casino where Paula worked when she came to Las Vegas for the first time and at twenty years of age.

"It's undergone a massive renovation recently. Do you want to see inside? I thought you might be interested."

He pulled her towards the entrance as he spoke.

"Sure, but Larry's not here. He's with Marie and they're visiting family in Montana."

Lachlan nodded in response. Larry was her special friend and he had worked with Paula back in those early days at the casino. His wife, Marie, was a close friend now and she was responsible for conducting the meditation group, which Paula attended weekly. The lady, Carol, who had been its co-ordinator originally, had moved away some time ago.

They entered the building and Paula's head swivelled from side-to-side as she attempted to recognise her old haunt. Everything was so very different. It bore little resemblance to her original workplace, so Lachlan had not exaggerated when he stated that it had undergone a massive change. He led her to the blackjack table. She knew that he would be unable to resist the temptation to play the game and she was not wrong in this assessment.

This had been the game that Paula had operated and she had loved every minute of it. Also, she had been very proficient in her chosen occupation back then.

As she watched Lachlan placing bets on the table, she became somewhat detached all of a sudden. She felt herself beginning to drift from her physical body almost immediately.

Without any effort on her part, she was hovering above her body while looking down on the area directly below her. The scene was one of frantic activity as many patrons worked extremely hard at enjoying themselves in the pursuit of money.

To Paula, in that moment, this resembled a kindergarten scene that she was observing. These were children at play. She could see their auras. Some were dark grey and murky. Others were displaying all of the different colours of the rainbow and these were intermingling as people brushed by one another, or stood side-by-side while being engrossed in the serious act of gambling and in the drinking of alcohol.

As quickly as it had occurred, the experience ceased for her and she was grounded again, being back in her body completely. She wondered at the scene that she had been witnessing for some time until the realisation dawned on her. She had been viewing everyone and everything from a parallel reality. Her physical body was here; but momentarily, she had been witnessing that scene in the casino from a very different perspective.

Were there two different and parallel realities operating side-by-side on the planet now, she pondered, as Lachlan placed another bet, after having lost the previous ones.

Paula recalled the writings that she had received from Gerard. Basically, this was what these were describing.

Up until this moment, she had seen Gerard's reality as being totally different and removed completely from this physical one. But, were they separate? Was one superimposed on the other, with the difference being simply that one operated on a slightly different frequency than the other? Therefore, those on the higher frequency would be able to watch those on the lower level while the ones with the lower vibration would be oblivious to ones who were observing them. That was a sobering thought, she acknowledged.

This was exactly how it had been for her when she was observing Lachlan at the hospital thirteen years earlier. Back then, he had been in the waiting room where the surgeon was speaking with him. He had been waiting for advice on her condition following the car accident. Her physical body was in a different section of the building at the time, because it was being removed from the operating theatre to the recovery unit while the two men were talking together.

Then, the doctor was revealing to Lachlan that Paula's life had been spared, but they were unable to save the baby that she was carrying.

What Paula had found remarkable was that she was able to see them clearly and in full, living colour as she stood beside Lachlan. Also, she could understand clearly all that the surgeon was imparting to him, regarding his wife's condition at that time. Paula had been there with the two men. On that fact, there was no doubt whatsoever, because she had been a silent witness.

Suddenly, Lachlan turned from the blackjack table. He swivelled around in disgust and he grabbed her arm. As he led her towards the main exit, he whispered in her ear.

"C'mon, let's get out of here. I don't know why I allowed you to drag me in here!"

"Yes, and you were kicking and screaming all the way, weren't you?" Paula retaliated.

He laughed in response. They walked the short distance to the restaurant.

Once seated at the table and with glasses of wine in front of them, he surprised her with a request.

"How about an Aussie Christmas on Gail's farm outside of Bendigo this year? How would you feel about that?"

"Australia? Are you suggesting we go back there this year?" Paula exclaimed, while frowning as she did so.

Lachlan nodded emphatically in response.

"Would you have any objections? We've spent many years visiting with your family in Tucson. It's time the girls were shown where their paternal grandmother spent her early years. Byron was Sophia's age the last time we were there."

Paula was silent as she contemplated his request. Gail was Lachlan's cousin and she had inherited the farm when her parents died. She had re-married recently, following a divorce from her former husband, Richard, several years earlier. She kept in close contact with Lachlan, Paula knew.

"This is very short notice," she replied.

"If I throw in a cruise on the mighty Murray River, would that tempt you? Who knows . . . you might even connect up with some old ghosts from times long past."

Instinctively, Paula gave a soft laugh. At the same time, she brought her shoe to within easy reach of his shin and she gave his leg a swift kick. She realised instantly that he was referring to the past-life scenario of Louisa and Charles Lyndhurst in Victoria, as well as on the paddle-steamers of the Murray River. This tale, she had revealed to him – wisely or otherwise – some years earlier. And now, he was baiting her.

Lachlan reached down and rubbed his leg.

"You'll pay for that!"

She glanced up to see the waiter approaching the table.

"This is a surprise request that's come out of the blue, darling. I hadn't considered returning to Australia ever again. Let me think on it," Paula requested.

"Well, not for too long, as I need to make bookings and to plan my schedules."

"Your schedules rule your life," Paula stated emphatically. "The girls would love it, I guess. Did this request come from Gail?"

In response, Lachlan nodded. The meal arrived. They were lost in their own thoughts for a time.

As they left the restaurant, Lachlan took Paula's hand. He appeared to be in a pensive mood.

"Come back to the office with me. I want to show you something."

They entered through the room that had been the living room once. From there, they moved to the area of the main bedroom, which was Lachlan's office now. Stephen was not present and they were alone. A framed print that Paula had given to Lachlan as a wedding gift was attached to the wall above his desk. It was a picture of a large sailing ship, with funnels that marked it as a steam vessel, also. The ship was alongside Port Melbourne pier and it depicted the vessel that Prince Alfred, the second son of Queen Victoria, had captained on the First Royal Tour of the Australian colonies in 1867.

Lachlan removed the picture and, behind it, there was a wall safe. Opening the safe, he extracted a small case, which he handed to Paula.

"This is not a gift for you. It's something I think you should see," he explained, in a soft tone.

On opening the jewellery case, she gasped in surprise.

"These are your mother's emeralds. Why did you remove them from the home safe and bring them here?" she asked, while being somewhat puzzled by his actions.

"No, they're not. These are identical to those and just as real, as well as being equally expensive as the original set."

"They're identical!" she exclaimed. "Why did you do that, Lachlan? Who on earth are they for?"

Paula was studying the jewellery in her hands. If he had not told her, she would not have known that these pieces were different from the set that had belonged to his mother. The original ones had been inherited by Marcia Jefferson on the death of her Australian grandmother many decades earlier. There was a large diamond and emerald necklace, a matching bracelet and a set of earrings, along with the wedding and engagement rings. No one seemed to know who the original owner had been.

Paula suspected that she did know the answer to that puzzle. She had not divulged the secret to anyone. She would be labelled as insane, if she were to be so unwise as to do so.

Paula had worn the original set on the night when they had enticed the confidence trickster, Lucas Britton, to the blackjack table during a gambling event held at a home, which Lachlan had leased on the Gold Coast in Australia. That had occurred almost a quarter of a century earlier.

Lachlan perched on the desk as she stood beside him and, holding the precious gems, she glanced at him.

"Why?" she queried him again. "Why go to the expense of buying another set? No one can wear the originals for fear of being attacked and robbed. They never come out of the safe at home as it is."

"Well, it started out as the simple purchase of an emerald here and a diamond there when I was travelling in Europe and elsewhere. Then, I had the idea to make another set, so that Sophia could have one, as the other jewellery is earmarked to be handed down to Melissa," Lachlan explained to Paula, in a soft, intimate tone before elaborating. "This collection just kept growing over the years. After that, I had to find a reputable jeweller and one whom I could trust to copy the original set perfectly. It needed to be someone who would not switch the precious stones I offered to him. I found one recently and he's done a great job. I've had this complete set valued. It's genuine and it's fully insured, as is Mom's set."

"Sophia is ten years old, for goodness sake! This is over the top, Lachlan!" Paula stated firmly. "You're besotted by the girls. They've wrapped you around their little fingers. Do they know about this?"

"No, Stephen is the one who I've trusted with this knowledge and that was in case you and I were taken from them suddenly, in one, foul swoop. It happened to Mom. It almost happened to you. So, I wanted our girls to have something tangible to carry them through any bad times that might come. Byron is well taken care of in that regard and I've made him fully aware of everything, as well as his responsibilities where the girls are concerned."

"Is something wrong? Is there something you're not telling me?" Paula asked, while being besieged by thoughts that he was leading to a dreaded disclosure of a medical nature.

"No, definitely not, and if it were so, do you think I'd wait for your birthday to break such news to you?"

Relief must have been evident on her face. He took the jewellery from her and he kissed her as he did so.

"The way this old world is going, I don't know what the future holds for any of us. If everything goes pear-shaped when they are older, they will have this jewellery to sell. It's insurance for them. That's all."

"What do you mean by that?"

He locked the safe and replaced the picture in front of it before he answered. She sat on his desk while awaiting his response. He was the most positive person that she knew, so she was surprised by this revelation. As he turned around, he brushed the hair back from his forehead in his usual manner that appeared when he was frustrated. Then, he grimaced.

"Think about it this way. When my mother grew up on the old farm in the back blocks of the Victorian countryside, way back in the early fifties, life was slow and time was measured by the rising and setting of the sun. All they had by way of outside communication was the radio. If they wanted to contact anyone in an emergency, they needed to ride a horse or drive an old farm vehicle a mile up the road to the corner store where there was a telephone box, which connected them to an operator for long distance calls. The world has changed so much in such a short period of time . . . in a little over sixty years, to be precise. Who knows where it's heading from here."

"Is this the reason you want to take the girls there?"

"Partly," Lachlan responded. "Byron has been to the farm and I can discuss things like this with him. He does seem to appreciate what I'm saying. But, the girls need to see the place and I want to explain to them what it was like when I visited it for the first time. I was only Sophia's age then."

"What do you mean when you talk about the way the world is going?"

"Paula, I'm involved in a business that is becoming more and more cut-throat with every day that passes. Everyone is out for what they can get. No one seems to care how that is done these days. There's no trust. A person's *word* doesn't count for anything anymore. There's no loyalty, no ethics and, most concerning of all, there's no time, especially for the niceties that were considered a necessary part of business life once. It's a dog-eat-dog world out there. There're wars and atrocities happening all over the place. There's no way the madness can go on, and especially not at the pace life is going. This can't continue indefinitely."

Lachlan lifted her from the desk and, with his arm around her shoulders, he guided her towards the door. As they left their old apartment, he murmured to her.

"I wile away hour-upon-hour in airport lounges all around the world. From my observations, people resemble robots that are on automatic pilot as they rush from place to place. Probably, I'm not much different from them. But, I do know this. Our world is changing rapidly. You'd have to be blind not to see it. All I'm attempting to do, with this jewellery as an example, is to cover all eventualities where our children are concerned. That's all." Lachlan stated, before explaining further. "Let's get you home. I've a crucial meeting this afternoon and it's likely to become an extremely nasty and fiery affair, so if I'm not at my best for your special day, I'm sorry. And, don't worry about the girls today, as Byron has promised to collect them from school later."

With those words, they headed in the direction of the car. Silence permeated the vehicle on the way home. He left her on the front porch where she remained as she watched his car disappearing down the long driveway at a very fast speed.

Lachlan had lived life at a very fast pace since the day that she had met him. Perhaps, this was a factor, which had led to his disclosures to her earlier at his Las Vegas office, and it was beginning to take its toll. It appeared to Paula that Lachlan Jefferson had been doing some very deep soul-searching of late.

Paula gave a quick wave to Jack, the gardener, as he tended to the plants in his usual fastidious manner. Jack and his wife, Carmel, who was their cook/housekeeper, lived in separate quarters at the rear of the house, along with their large colony of pampered cats. This was an arrangement that suited everyone perfectly. The small garden area, which Jack had created, provided a peaceful and beautiful oasis in their desert hideaway.

With a deep sigh, she turned away. It was a very pensive Paula who entered their home this day.

Chapter Three

Paula went immediately to her meditation room, but Lachlan's revelations to her in his office a little earlier were troubling her deeply. She walked to the divan in the corner of the room where she retrieved her jacket from there. The air conditioning was quite cool after the warmth of the sunshine in the garden. She slipped the jacket around her shoulders.

As she did so, she stood by the window while gazing out at the great expanse of desert stretched before her. She recalled the strange sensation of drifting out of her body while visiting the old casino today and how she had been floating above the scene that was occurring in the building. The experience had been as surreal as it had been unexpected.

Her world with Gerard was a separate reality. She crossed a suspension bridge to reach there. On other occasions, she had walked through an old, disused railway tunnel and she arrived in his world. Today's unexpected experience had been different in that she did not make a definite decision to visit another realm, as occurred during her deliberate meditation sessions.

So, why had this happened today at the casino, she queried softly to herself. Was that other reality edging ever closer to the physical one, without most people being aware of this occurrence at a conscious level?

The massive structure where Gerald had taken her recently and inside of which she had experienced the most intoxicating feelings of love and peace, appeared real to her when she was there with him. In fact, it was so real that she never wanted to leave its sanctuary. It possessed twelve separate and distinct entrances. He referred to the building as the *Holy-of-Holies* – *The New Jerusalem*.

Prior to today's experience in the casino, she had viewed the massive structure, known as *The New Jerusalem*, as being in another place entirely. What if, she pondered, this other reality was edging ever closer to the physical one. What if it was super-imposed already on the physical world and, at another deeper level within ourselves, we knew of its existence? Would this cause people to rush around faster and faster in ever-decreasing circles as they sought desperately to hold onto the illusionary, physical existence that they had created for themselves and in which they felt relatively safe in this physical world on Earth?

"Perhaps, it is so," Paula murmured aloud, as these never-ending thoughts persisted. "Maybe, the *New Jerusalem* has arrived already on the planet and no one wants to know about it. How very sad that would be!"

Her experiences there were so real and so awe-inspiring that to have it as a permanent place of residence – a conscious reality – where everyone could abide in peace, tranquillity and unconditional love permanently was a precious dream. Would this really become a definite reality on Earth in the not-too-distant future, she queried herself.

With a deep sigh, she shrugged her shoulders imperceptibly as she turned from the window.

She sat at her desk and opened the folder containing the Discourses. She located the section that she had been reading before Lachlan disturbed her earlier in the day.

She did not begin reading immediately. Lachlan's words came back to her and these continued to haunt her. She wondered what had precipitated them. Perhaps, it was the business meeting, which he had looming this afternoon that was upsetting him. However, if someone with Lachlan's hectic lifestyle, busy business commitments and totally positive outlook on life had begun to notice the sorry state, to which this world had descended currently, the situation was grave indeed, she mused. Tomorrow would be the eleventh anniversary of the September 11 attacks on America. Nothing had been the same since that time when all innocence was lost.

Perhaps, the moment had arrived for the release of these Discourses, she murmured softly. Turning the page over, she began to read the words again. A short time later, she reached for a pen to write an introduction to the Discourses.

As she concluded the short passage, she had the distinct feeling that she was being observed. Turning, she saw Lachlan standing in the doorway of her meditation room. In slight confusion, she frowned as she spoke to him.

"Hello, darling, did you forget something?"

Lachlan laughed and shook his head as he gazed at her.

"What planet are you on this time? It's two hours since I left you at the front door."

He came to her and, reaching for her hands, he removed the pen and placed it on the desk. Lifting her gently from the chair, he placed his arms around her.

"Where're the girls?" Paula queried.

"Don't worry. They're quite safe and with Byron. He's taking them to their Uncle Stephen who has promised to take good care of them, so that I can spend some time alone with my wife and bring my gift to her. If Stephen delivers them home here in under two hours, he will be unemployed by tomorrow. *And,* I'll wring his neck, just for good measure," Lachlan stated emphatically, before placing his two hands on either side of her face. "Now, do you have any objections to this arrangement, Paula Elizabeth Jefferson?"

Before she could reply, he kissed her.

"None whatsoever, Mr. Jefferson," she murmured, as he released her face momentarily while beginning to manoeuvre her body backwards slowly in the direction of the divan in the corner of the room.

"I love you so much," he whispered. "You're my anchor; do you know that? Wherever I am in the world, it takes but one tiny tug on the anchor rope and I'm back here in your arms."

"I love you, too . . . and oh-so-much. I couldn't exist without you, Lachlan," Paula murmured, as her arms encircled his body.

The deep love that they had shared together, down through all the ages-of-time, consumed them then.

It was the same love that consumed Fiona and Alexander during their short but tragic life together in the Highlands of Scotland and, most especially so, on their wedding night as, beneath the gentle rays of a watery moon, they had consummated their union on the banks of the river, which later claimed Fiona's life, in the year of 1745.

It was the same love that consumed Louisa and Charles during their short time together in Victorian Victoria and, most especially so, on the night when, finally, Louisa gave herself freely and without reservation to Charles as a wild and fierce thunder storm lashed their Melbourne home in 1868.

It was the same love that consumed them when they possessed the identities of Paula and Lachlan and, most especially so now, while living together in their secluded, desert hideaway on the outskirts of Las Vegas in 2012.

Whether inhabiting different physical forms, being in different countries and cultures, possessing different identities and accepting different religious beliefs, concepts and/or philosophies, these two lovers come together time after time, but always with the same person-alities, the same predictable mannerisms and emotional responses to situations and with similar attitudes to life.

And always, without fail, they fall deeply in love all over again, without having conscious recall back to all of the other times when this totally-addictive and all-consuming passion swamped them completely in its tidal wave of uncompromising and unconditional love.

Beyond the grave and for all eternity, these two lovers are bound to each other. They are inextricably linked by bonds that are so strong that no force on Earth or elsewhere could break or sever their connection, as well as their commitment, to each other. How could such a bond be broken?

In other realms, they are known by other names. They are Twin Flames there, beyond the suspension bridge, between two realms and everywhere in-between, including wherever that they choose to wander in their world of Love unbridled, Love unconditional and Love unbounded and unlimited.

They are – always have been and forever will be – *Selene* and *Gerard!*

The Series

Finally and with great reluctance, we leave Paula and Lachlan to live out the rest of their lives together, along with their young, lively and beautiful family. Perhaps, this time around, they will manage to live happily-ever-after. This is assuming, of course, that world events do not intervene to interfere with their own perfectly pre-planned life-span in this current earthly life-experience.

Let us hope that this is the case and that they spend many a happy moment in each other's company.

When I watched the movie, which was released not long ago and that was entitled *AVATAR*, I was struck by the similarities of what I was attempting to present here with Paula and her time-travelling experiences – real or imagined. In the movie, the character, Jake, was interacting in two different realities, as Paula has been doing since the accident in 1999.

When Paula was communicating with Gerard, during her meditation sessions, it was similar to when Jake was operating in another reality, which was different from his current one. As with Paula, he had conscious recall in both places. However, with Paula, when she was interacting with Gerard on that other plane of existence during sleep – or, in her dream-state, as Gerard referred to it – she did not remember anything that had occurred during her time with Gerard in those instances.

Undoubtedly, she would have been given clear guidance on what she needed to do when she returned to the lower physical reality, but she would not remember the details consciously when she opened her eyes in her physical body in the morning. So, she had to rely on her in-built directional compass, guidance system or intuition, depending on one's interpretation.

With Jake of *AVATAR* fame, he received instruction and advice when he came out of his sleep-state. Some of it came from ones who had the interests of the native inhabitants of Pandora in the forefront of their minds. Others were giving him definitely negative instructions.

This, of course, was not happening with Paula. She was given only loving guidance at all times when she was in Gerard's reality. She possesses free will. Whether or not she walks in and operates in love only when she is in her physical world, is her free will choice, just as the character, Jake, had a free will choice with regard to the actions that he chose to take when interacting with the native population of the planet where he was visiting.

With the inhabitants of Pandora, they were the ones who were more in-tune with the energy and essence flowing in and around them constantly. They were, in fact, the ones who were operating on the higher vibratory frequencies while the ones who were attempting to exploit and destroy them were the ones who were operating on the lower vibratory frequency. That was my assessment of the situation.

As with the current inhabitants of Earth, it is our choice as to whether we decide to emulate and embrace the negative philosophy of some of the rulers of Earth, in every sphere of everyday life; or, if we decide to emulate and embrace the higher ideals and higher frequencies of a more enlightened and loving community.

Pandora was saved and her loving inhabitants lived to rebuild their lives and communities. Will this happen on Earth? Or, is it already too late to reverse the situation? I suppose that this will depend on how many of her inhabitants can raise their own vibratory frequency in a short space of time to bring about a miracle such as that enormous one.

Basically, this is what these Discourses in Part Two of this book cover and in plain and direct language.

In the movie, Jake kept a video diary. Is this any different to us keeping a video diary of every lifetime that we have ever lived on Earth and storing that video diary in a library somewhere that is called the *Akashic Records?* Perhaps, these fictitious stories are not all that far-fetched after all. It was into this video diary of a former life that Paula was delving while her body was on the operating table in the Gold Coast Hospital.

During the space of these two trilogies, we have watched her as she reviewed her former lifetimes in eighteenth century Scotland and nineteenth century Australia, as well as an earlier period of her life in America in the twentieth century.

Paula has learned much since the car accident. She has witnessed the world about her changing drastically. The last traces of innocence were lost with the horrific terrorists attacks of 2001. From her new perspective, she can see these changes occurring. During her meditation sessions, she can cross the suspension bridge and, from there, she can view the overall picture from outside the rim of Earth. It is not a pretty picture.

In everyday life, often it is easier for us to pretend that our world is not changing and so, we can go on with our ordinary, fast-paced lives as though there is no tomorrow while reiterating to ourselves that there is no need for change at all. With the constantly-increasing natural disasters that are happening, can anyone believe this to be so?

The Discourses are presented in Part Two for those who wish to ponder further on these matters. Some were released in the earlier books of the Series. However, these are included here, also, for those who are interested in their content.

In Meditation

I n the book, **ERA of DISCERNMENT**, I included a meditation guide for the contemplation of anyone who was wishing to start out on this pathway. It was given as an initial guide only, especially where planetary healing was concerned. Many excellent books on the subject of meditation have been published previously and are available for those who are interested in the topic. Getting started is the most difficult part. After that, it is simply a matter of experimenting to find the most appropriate method that seems to be suitable for the one who is embarking on the process.

At the time of the earthquake, tsunami and subsequent nuclear disaster in Japan, I asked the following questions during a deep meditation session. On the following morning when I awoke, I received an answer to those questions. I wrote down the explanation that came clearly into my mind. I will give the questions and answers here. Whether or not these are correct is for the reader to decide. Perhaps, the Discourses, which appear in Part Two of this book, will enlighten further.

Questions to ponder:

(a)

Why are there so many natural disasters occurring on Earth at present?

(b)

Why do not the leaders of Earth – self-appointed and/or elected – have the answers to these events?

(c)

Why do not the great scientific minds of Earth – the elite group of well-respected scientists – have the answers, with regard to the advanced timing and the location where these events will occur?

Answer:

'On Earth today, there are many who are struggling to understand these events and why they are happening. Some blame climate change. Others blame other factors, such as a mass turning-away from organised religions. Most do not recognise that Earth is a living, breathing Creation of the Mother-Father-God-Principle. All the great scientific minds of Earth today could not work collectively to reproduce such a beautiful Creation as this planet is – or was. She is not just the rock beneath the feet of humankind. She is the life-source for all who walk on her surface and who take her for granted daily, in most cases. Earth is hurting. She is hurting badly.

With the dawning of Aquarius, few realise the immense damage that has been done to the Earthly Mother over the past centuries. With an understanding of reincarnation comes the realisation that perhaps ones who orchestrated these atrocities previously, are back in charge again now. They could be in different bodies, with different identities, but they are the same ones who raped her previously – for their own selfish gain and to appease their greed. They will never relinquish that control voluntarily. They form dynasties and conglomerates to make certain that their legacy of destruction continues. But, it cannot continue on into the New Age of Aquarius. They will fight tooth-and-nail to hold onto their power. They cannot live without that power. They pulse only to the vibration of the Sacral chakra, which is the centre of Divine Power. They will never relinquish *the power* of their own volition. They see it as their birthright and they will destroy anyone – financially, personally, politically and/ or physically – if that person is so unwise as to attempt such an impossible feat.

If all of the mining for minerals, for oil and for gas were to cease immediately – on this fourth day of April, in the year 2011 – it would be too late to repair the damage that has been done to the Earthly Mother.

Why is this statement made? It is because, during the two thousand year cycle of Aquarius, the planet will not survive. The *Rock* beneath the feet of those who call Earth *home* is dying slowly. That wondrous Creation of God Whom few recognise as her Architect is gasping now. She needs time to recuperate. She needs *time-alone* to rejuvenate and to regenerate. She cannot do so while such degradation of her surface and her inner-parts is allowed to continue. Her inner regions are similar to the inner regions and organs of the physical body. This is not a fact that is universally-recognised or accepted.

Unfortunately, in order to save the Earthly Mother, a set of principles will need to be put in place. Those who fight against these principles – and most will do so – will be the first to leave the planet via the death experience. They will face then the facts, regarding their own involvement in Earth's demise over many centuries. Their Akashic Records will be on display for all to view and they will hang their heads in deep shame as their selfish motives are revealed.

The children who work and walk only in Divine Love and Divine Light, regardless of their religious beliefs or their political affiliations, will have another chance to take up the reins as Earth tries to heal, as well as to repair the damage that has been done to her already.

It was hoped, at the outset, that this would have been accomplished during the past Piscean Age. But, this was not achieved. So, it is necessary to force this healing process onto Earth's inhabitants now, so as to save the planet from destruction. There is no other course of action that is more important than this one is currently.

The planet is dying. *She is a living, breathing example of the Mother-Father-God-Principle.*

She is in severe distress. She is in her death throes now as a third dimensional planet.

Mother Earth is convulsing!'

Part Two

Discourses

Introduction to the Discourses
The White Lighthouse

When Paula followed her Guide, Gerard, up the steps inside the white lighthouse, she did not know or understand why she was doing so. She was in a deep meditative state and she followed him in complete trust. So, where was he taking her and what was he attempting to reveal to her during this visit? He was holding a candle in a candle holder as he mounted the circular metal steps. He was dressed in a long, white robe.

Gerard was endeavouring to bring Paula to an understanding of the need for self-healing. Through self-healing, it is possible to clear one's auric field and to raise the vibratory frequency of all of the bodies, which are encased within and around the physical one. If the physical one is suffering, due to wear-and-tear or other ailments, the time has come to heal it at the deepest level. Paula – as with almost everyone else on the planet – has forgotten why she came down into physical embodiment at this time. She came, first and foremost, to clear her *stuff*, as many term this terrible, but necessary, chore.

So, how does she do so and where does she begin? For those who have read my book, **UNDERCOVER STARSEEDS**, which was published in 2002, the understanding for this need will be obvious. By taking Paula up those stairs in the lighthouse, Gerard was revealing just one possibility to her on how to begin the task. Where she begins is a matter for her own Higher Self to determine, assuming that the (Higher) Spirit Self is given permission by the one in embodiment – that being the little soul-spirit – to do so. It is oh-so-simple.

There is no need to rely on others. Of course, there are many wonderful healers who are working at the etheric/Astral level, in order to assist those who are open to receive these higher energies. But, once again, this is a personal journey. Whoever, or whatever, the seeker needs to assist in this endeavour will come to that person in the appropriate time. Going-it-alone, by utilising the method outlined here, would be an excellent way to commence. After that, an occasional visit to an established and genuine healer may assist in accelerating the releasing, clearing and healing process. This is an individual choice, of course.

On the first level of the lighthouse, Gerard ignited several candles and this revealed an area where one could visit for a time, during a deep meditation session. Handing over the reins to the Higher Self, at this stage, would be helpful. The area was **Red** in colour, so we are at the area of the **Base** (or Root) chakra here. There are many excellent publications that outline the problems, which can be associated with a blockage of this particular energy centre. Perhaps, some of those publications can be listed at the end of this introduction for the benefit of those who wish to have a greater understanding of these matters. To be brief, health issues associated with this energy centre would arise if the chakra – which has been described previously as being a wheel-within-a-wheel – was not functioning as normal and/or it was out-of-balance. This wheel-within-a-wheel description is an apt one.

If the centre is shrouded in negative energy, for example, due to a past-life experience and from a trauma in this current lifetime, the centre could be partially closed or spinning in reverse. If this were to be the case, an illness or a disease may have manifested itself already in this area.

Let us refer to these chakras or energy centres as **Points** from here onwards to avoid confusion. There are many of these Points within the body. Some are minor and some are major. There are seven major ones that affect the physical body. Above the Crown of the head, there are two more Points. Below the minor ones in the feet, there are two more major ones in existence. So, let us give them all titles.

Commencing at the bottom of the auric field, there is the **Omega Point**. Closer to the feet comes the **Ground Point**.

Then, we have the minor chakras in the feet and in the knees. The next major one is the **Base Point**, which is **Red** in colour. This is where Gerard began his teaching exercise for Paula, on the first level of the lighthouse. Here, everything in sight was red. This is the Point of **Divine Life**.

On the next level in the lighthouse, everything appeared as the colour **Orange**. This is the **Sacral Point**. This is the Point of **Divine Power**.

Following on from this one, Paula arrived at a higher level that was bathed in **Yellow**. It is the **Solar Plexus Point**, the centre of Balance. This is the Point of **Divine Order**.

At a higher level still, she came to the area that was glowing with a **Green** colour. This is the **Heart Point**. This is the Point of **Divine Love**.

Climbing higher still within the lighthouse, we reach the level that is bathed in **Blue Light**. This is the **Throat Point**, the centre of communication. This is the Point of **Divine Will**.

Above the level of the throat, we have another area and this one is glowing with a **Purple** colour. This is the **Third Eye Point**. This is the Point of **Divine Wisdom**.

Higher still within our illusionary lighthouse, we have a section that is glowing with the colour of **Indigo**. It is the **Crown Point**. This is the Point of **Divine Light**.

Above the Crown Point, we reach the area of the **Star Point**.

The Point, at this height, is **Pulsing** with a **Golden/White Light**.

To reach this vibratory frequency, while inhabiting a physical body, is to achieve *Self-Mastery* at an incredible, unbelievable level. This is an almost-impossible feat. Only the most enlightened, dedicated and great Ascended Masters of Light arise to these dizzy heights while in embodiment on Earth. This is the level of **The Buddha**. This is the level of **The Christ**. An accomplishment such as this one is virtually unattainable whilst in physical form.

Ones who achieve even higher – thereby reaching the greatest and most astounding level of the **Alpha Point** – are able to say, with genuine sincerity, the words:

"I AM THE ALPHA AND THE OMEGA!"

FOOTNOTE:

Perhaps, with this explanation, the poem, **ETERNAL CALL**, may be understood more easily. This poem is published here, as well as on my website: www.stellamcmillan.com.au

The original White Lighthouse meditation appeared in the fifth book of the Series, **ERROR PROFOUND.**

Three publications that may offer increased insight for those wishing to pursue further these spiritual understandings, especially with regard to self-healing, are listed here.

Hands of Light

Light Emerging

Barbara Ann Brennan

The Creation of Health

C. Norman Shealy M.D. Ph.D. & Caroline M Myss, M.A.

These are but the tip-of-the-iceberg as far as easily accessible, spiritual writings are concerned – in this, our long-awaited **ERA of DISCERNMENT.**

Discourse 1

The Power of Crystals

In a matter of moments, one knows exactly what one is meant to be doing in any given sphere of existence. For example, when one is a healer who devotes much time, effort and energy to the healing of others, that person knows intuitively what to do and when to do so. However, in the physical realm where often the ego-personality self is in control fully, then one could be of two minds, so to speak. This occurs because the ego-self is demanding, through its conscious mind, that a certain course of action be taken immediately, while the soft, gentle, kind and loving Voice of Spirit-Within – coming through one's own spirit-self – may be guiding that another course of action be taken.

When a healer is working spiritually, often stones known as crystals – that are rocks, which Mother Earth has formed and fashioned herself – are utilised to aid in this process. When these crystals are placed on certain chakras, or energy centres, of the body, then a beam of Healing Energy and Love Essence is directed by the healer to that chakra; then, much healing occurs at an etheric and at an Astral level within the finer bodies of the patient. Presumably, prior to the commencement of the session, the patient and the healer have asked their own, individual I AM Presence/Higher Self for assistance, for guidance, for protection and for the active participation of each one in the healing process that is taking place on a healing table in the physical world.

The stones/crystals to be utilised will be selected by the healer, following intuitively the Guidance that is coming from their own I AM Presence. The wise selection of these crystals will determine the colour of the stone chosen for every chakra. Every energy centre within the body requires a different colour, just as every ailment requires a different solution, depending on which organ of the physical body is affected by the disease that is being treated currently in the session.

Often, this is not understood by ones participating in these activities on Earth, even though they are doing so from a purely unselfish perspective and they are doing wonderful work anyway. Sometimes, there may be several stones needed for the same chakra, while another energy centre may require one crystal only – that being the one whose colour corresponds with the colour of the chakra involved. From our perspective in Spirit, it is simple. With a little understanding and a few tips given through writings such as these, more understanding will come to the healers as they progress with their work.

The most important factor is the Love Aspect. That point cannot be stressed sufficiently strongly. It is helpful, also, to note that whatever is affecting negatively the Astral Body, etheric body, mental and/or emotional body must become apparent eventually within the physical body – hence the saying: 'as above, so below'. This manifests itself as an illness or ailment of some description. How severe this problem is for the patient is related directly to what caused the original injury that would have occurred in a past-life situation, one would assume, and how long the problem was festering there before the patient sought treatment for the complaint.

So, there is a brief outline on the use of crystals as they apply to healing. Of course, they do have many other more practical uses, such as within the mechanisms of time pieces/watches and computers and this but scratches the surface of their benefits, although time does not permit a full disclosure of these applications at the moment.

Peace be with you as my Love enfolds you now.

Discourse 2

Twin Flames

(From the sixth book, *ERA of DISCERNMENT*)

Upon your earth-plane of existence, there appears from time-to-time sets of twins who are so in-tune with each other that even rational minds within the medical fraternity are forced to sit up and take notice. For example, two sisters who are born within minutes of each other, who never marry, who devote their entire lives to each other and who, when one begins a sentence while speaking, the other will finish that sentence. It is as though they have but one mind and the same thought enters both minds at the same moment.

This is a very poor comparison where Twin Flames are concerned. A Twin Flame is but one half of the equation. Twin Flames were birthed into existence as the One-Being by our Loving Creator-God aeons ago. As everyone and everything within God's great universes is pulsing with God's Love, while contracting and expanding with God's Light, then growth is inevitable for most. In order to grow in understanding, faith and Love, a Bubble-of-Light, after its birth, separates as does an egg that appears to have a double-yoke. It is only one egg still, but it has two halves. This is an analogy that could be applied to the Twin Flames explanation.

When Twin Flames come back together, they can create anything they wish, for they are very powerful Beings-of-Light and Love. However, for the most part, they remain separate, because each one has his/her own path to walk. Were they to come together in physical form on Earth, for example, then they would achieve very little as far as physical growth or spiritual growth is concerned, because they would be so absorbed totally in each other and in the welfare of their other half, that they would neglect to do all that was planned prior to that incarnation. It is somewhat like the twins mentioned above, as one half of the pair would become so dependent upon and reliant on its other part of itself that little could or would be accomplished.

Of course, there have been occasions when this has occurred on Earth and remarkable achievements have taken place as a result. Usually though, this is when a particular event needs to take place – one perhaps that will change the destiny of humankind – and then, the ones who incarnate are usually great Masters of Light in their own right, so they are equal to the challenges that life presents to them. More often than not, prior to incarnation, these Twin Flames will come to an agreement as to which one will play the dominate role in the partnership and which one will play the supporting role in the unfolding drama being acted out by the two during the forthcoming Earth embodiments. As they are of 'one mind' at all times, this is possible.

So, this is the answer to why ones on Earth, in any incarnation and during any time-frame – past or present – will seek endlessly for that 'one, true love'. It is because they are seeking to find their own Twin Flame, for then and only then, is a perfect union possible. However, the truth of the matter is that this search is fruitless. This is due to the fact that Twin Flames incarnate on Earth rarely at the same time. If they did so – and even if they chose different continents, different religions, different languages and a different race, to which to belong – they would find each other still. The magnetic attraction within their own energy fields would be so powerful that they would find their way to each other to become the One-Being again for a time. Trying to keep them separate on a planet as small as Earth is, would be similar to holding two halves of the same horse-shoe shaped magnet together in the palm of one hand and expecting them to stay apart from each other. It cannot be done. This would be a complete impossibility.

Perhaps, with this in mind, one can understand the great and sometimes urgent need that people have to find the 'perfect mate' while in embodiment. What they do not understand is why it is not possible. So, they meet up with other members of their own very extensive soul-family and they choose a mate from these ones, whom they know and love so well when resting and recuperating between incarnations on the Astral plane of Spirit. Also, of course, they have had many different incarnations together on Earth and, as a result, they have forged great bonds of understanding, respect, love and, in many cases, have had total commitment to each other, until death did them part. Then, when that identity concluded for one, the other became distraught and often was totally lost, when left alone on Earth.

So it is then that when they meet up again in a subsequent incarnation, the *tie or cord-of-attachment* is very strong already and they come together automatically, because they know each other so very well and love each other deeply, regardless of earthly barriers to their love and subsequent union.

They would not meet up by accident either, for there are no such occurrences. They plan their relationships together, for the most part, before incarnating; but, always on Earth, there is free will and, sometimes despite the best of intentions and the most careful planning, one of those involved in the proposed partnership may decide to take a different course once in embodiment. This, then, leaves the other party somewhat high and dry, one might say. The reasons that they planned to come together originally could be many and varied but, usually, it is because they have major issues of dispute, which have occurred previously on Earth and that require a loving resolution. However, when in Spirit form, there are no differences, because all are living, working and playing in Love.

On Earth, it is the ego-personality self (as opposed to the spirit-self) who is in charge, for the most part, and this is where and when differences and difficulties arise. The ironing-out of these problems and the dispensing of any outstanding karmic debt that may have accrued over several lifetimes, due to these outstanding issues, is why the relationship is planned, for the most part.

These ones, who are the chosen life-partners in an Earth encounter, are referred to as soul-mates usually. Sometimes, if these partnerships are ongoing for lifetime after lifetime, some may choose to call these situations 'twin-souls'. Twin-souls and Twin Flames are completely different. A twin-soul can never, ever become the Twin Flame of their life-partner, no matter how many times they choose to incarnate together.

So, here we conclude the explanation about Twin Flames. Twin Flames were breathed into Life together as the One-Being. There will come a time-of-reconnection when they will become *The One* again. Until that blessed moment, they will continue to learn, to grow and to mature as they continue their quest for understanding, enlightenment and Truth Everlasting.

There can be no greater quest!

In God's Love, I leave you. *Adieu.*

Discourse 3

Relationships –Ties/Cords of Attachment

Having covered the topic of Twin Flames, let us consider two other topics that may have arisen here in these Discourses so far. One of these is the very thorny issue of *relationships*. The other one that has been touched on briefly is that of *ties or cords of attachment* to ones, with whom we have had different relationships over thousands upon thousands of earth-years. Just by studying a brief chart of ones who have been involved in any ongoing drama over but two or three life-cycles, we can see how these connections continue endlessly.

Consider how many lifetimes that you have had with your current husband or partner. Often, you know exactly what he or she will say and how that person will react in any given situation. Why do you think that this is so? The person has not only been your husband/ partner. He has been your father, your grandfather, your mother and your sibling, in the form of a younger sister, whom you have cared for upon the death of your mother – as an example. Also, there have been occasions when you have been secret lovers while married to other partners. So, you see, you have a very chequered history – the two of you. You know each other very well indeed and this is not surprising when seen from a higher perspective. And, that is how all of these issues need to be contemplated in order to achieve the level of understanding and enlightenment that you seek so desperately now in your state of heightened *Awareness*.

As with all who inhabit physical bodies currently on Earth, you have free will and you have the right to choose whether you will open your eyes wider still and view the larger canvas from this higher perspective or Higher Consciousness; or, you can continue to wear 'blinkers' or 'blinders', as do the race horses who rush forward and race ahead on the track, without looking from side-to-side, purely out of fear – a fear of what they might 'see' and of what might distract them from the relentless pursuit forward to the finishing line and, hopefully, success in their physical existence.

It is fear, therefore, that will prevent many people from accepting reincarnation as a fact-of-life. However, the craziness in all of this is that no one knows, at a conscious level, the moment of his or her own death in any incarnation. Yet, at the precise moment of death in every incarnation, one acknowledges this fact instantly, because the first happening, after the acknowledgement that death – in all its finality – has occurred, is that clarity-of-thought returns. The spirit-self takes charge fully and the ego-personality self takes a back seat, so to speak. Then, the person concerned exclaims: "Oh! No! Not again . . . how could I have been so blind *once again?*"

No one, in current physical form on Earth, has been immune from death in the past and nor will they be in the present time. Everyone, without exception, has moved beyond that thin veil of illusion, known as the death experience hundreds and hundreds of times; yet still, they continue to maintain, especially in the western world, that reincarnation is a complete impossibility. There is such an abject fear of death and a fear of acknowledging one's own physical mortality, that merely to discuss such a subject, even in passing, is taboo.

Fear – fear of the unknown – is the main reason. Another reason is that many people have difficulty in accepting that they may have wronged others in this lifetime and a karmic debt may have been the result. And so it is that they cannot contemplate such a preposterous suggestion as the one that there could be other outstanding karmic debts from past-life experiences. It is easier to tighten the blinders on one's eyes and to carry on regardless, while ridiculing such suggestions emphatically.

We can watch kindergarten children at play in their playground. This is their very miniature world. Outside of that miniature world is a world, which is peopled by adults who marvel at the antics and the innocence of these blessed little ones at play. Yet, they themselves resemble children at play while living in the world of the physical, as they refuse to acknowledge or accept that anything outside of their small playground, known as Planet Earth, could possibly exist.

In their minds, Earth is all that there is. In all of the great universes controlled by Divine Power and fuelled by the Divine Love of Almighty God – the Power, Majesty and Love behind the Great Central Sun of Creation – Earth is the only one that has life. Earth is the only one where all life stops at the moment when one meets physical death face-to-face. Is such a preposterous suggestion possible? No, of course, it is not, except to those who continue to dwell in a world-of-denial and who wear blinders at all times, so that they cannot see anything beyond the world of illusion, which they have created for their own protection and in which they live in fear, ignorance and darkness caused by dense negativity.

In order to continue this world of illusion, they form relationships with others of like-mind. They procreate to keep the species – this being the human race – alive. Within these relationships are cords that bind one to another for lifetime after lifetime after lifetime. So, when ones who have been together previously in past incarnations, come together again, it is as though they are meeting for the first time. It is due solely to the illusion that has been created and that is being perpetuated by ones who have a vested interest in so doing.

As every *new* relationship develops, old habits or patterns that are locked away tightly within the memory-field of those cords-of-attachments begin to unravel and to surface. Some patterns may be positive. Some patterns may be negative. But, all of these need to be balanced, at least. The ultimate goal is to release, clear, cleanse and heal them completely. Through studying various past-life situations, we can witness the old habits and patterns of previous lifetimes shared with others as these re-emerged in our current lives.

On Earth, there is a saying, which suggests that you must cut another free, so that the person concerned is as free as a bird in the sky. Then, should that person return to the one who is doing the releasing – and do so of his or her free will – the two are meant to be together. This is how it is with these cords-of-attachment. They bind you together, beyond the illusion of the death experience, and so you can never be free to become your own person and to walk your own path in life when you are being pulled this way and that way by others. In the severing of these ties, there is no lessening of the love that one has for the other. This would not be possible.

Think of all of the people who you have been with in every incarnation. I speak now of all – parents, peers, friends, offspring, siblings and acquaintances. For everyone that has touched you, at a heart level, there is a connection – a cord or tie of attachment. Your own next-door neighbour now may have been someone whom you cared about so deeply in a past-life that you descended into the deepest depression at his/her passing; whereas, today, you have but a nodding acquaintance, shall we say, and I speak hypothetically here, of course. But, even so, if this were to be the case, there would be a cord of attachment in place between the two of you. How is it possible then for anyone on the earth-plane to walk his or her own individual pathway back to God when others are dictating the terms while telling the person concerned how a life should be lived? It is not possible, so these cords must be severed. All of the debris from all of those past experiences held and locked securely in the vault of the subconscious mind and stored deeply in your soul-memory must be released into the Light so that all negativity can be dissipated and you can move on with your pathway to enlightenment.

However, there is sufficient negativity on Earth now, without releasing more into the atmosphere, would you not agree? After the releasing and the clearing comes the healing. All this can be carried out with great assistance from your own Higher Self, who is your permanent identity. Everyone has a permanent identity. It is who they are when not playing out their roles in physical embodiment where they have a temporary identity during the course of a particular lifetime. Your Higher Self cannot release, clear, cleanse and heal at a deep level for you unless you ask specifically for this to occur, because the free will factor comes into play.

So, ask and you will receive always. But, it is very wise to do so in a controlled environment – where you have full control of the situation and where no one can disturb you at this time. If you wish to utilise the services of one who is working as a healer, who is reputable and who is not charging 'the earth' for those services, this is an excellent way to proceed, especially for ones who are starting out on this pathway of self-healing. For most healers, this is regarded as their service.

These beautiful ones-of-Light may be utilising Reiki, crystal healing, spiritual healing, or a combination of all of these methods. The healer can do so only with your permission and with the permission of your Higher Self. Remember that *Free Will* is your birthright.

Free will was a gift given to you at the moment of Creation – your own Creation when you were birthed into life as another Bubble-of-Pure-Light and Pure Love – and it is sacrosanct. The greatest gift that you can give to your Creator-God is to hand back your free will, with those few precious words: "Not my will, dear God, but Thy Will be done!"

If all of the great prophets of Light who have walked the Earth before us could do so, why is it so difficult for the remainder of the population to utter these words, with meaning and with deep feeling? The answer is that the ego-personality self is not prepared to hand the control of one's life, when in embodiment, to the precious spirit-self within, who is Pure Light and Pure Love.

Always remember that: *Spirit is soft. Spirit is gentle. Spirit is kind. Spirit is loving.*

At all times, Spirit is soft, gentle, kind and loving. Know that all else comes from the ego-personality self.

Try to follow this guidance, so that in this way and at the appointed moment, you will *Come Home* in Light and Love, as well as in Higher Consciousness and in True Understanding and Enlightenment.

Peace be with you. *Adieu.*

Author's Comment

Paula's transformation was coming to her slowly when we left her at the conclusion of the story of her current life. Unfortunately, it had taken a major and very painful upheaval in her life to bring her to this understanding and to draw her back onto her pre-chosen spiritual pathway.

Who was it that arranged this major turn-around? It was her Higher Self, Selene, acting in conjunction with her own little spirit-self.

At a conscious level, her ego-personality self was unaware of this arrangement. However, after the event, free will was in play still. Paula could have chosen to follow the dictates of her ego-self, thereby returning to her old, fast-paced lifestyle that she was enjoying in Los Angeles prior to the accident.

Instead, she chose the more difficult road to self-discovery while walking blindfold as she listened to the suggestions and guidance coming softly but directly from her intuitive self, rather than following blindly the dictates of her ego-personality self. That is the difference.

With these three consecutive lifetimes, she has gravitated towards Lachlan, regardless of the identity that each one was carrying in previous times. They have been drawn to each other in all of these lifetimes in a similar manner to the attraction that exists between the moth and the flame. Regardless of the problems that arise in their relationship, in every lifetime, they are tied to each other through a great bond of love that has stood the test of time and physical death.

Discourse 4

Gaia

She is hurting. She is desperate. She cannot survive unless the ones who rape her daily and nightly are stopped.

Gaia has called out to God for help. In her distress and her pain, she has pleaded for help. She has pleaded for Divine Intervention.

Her waterways are polluted beyond what it is possible for humanity collectively to redress. Her air is polluted beyond belief.

Her tremors cause fear on Earth. Her tremors are her fears expressed in the only way that she knows how to express herself to the children who walk upon her surface.

Her storms are becoming more violent and more frequent as she attempts to attract the attention of a humanity that is steeped in selfishness and oblivious to her needs.

Her anger at the treatment, which she receives at the hands of the children who reside on her currently, is beyond boiling point. Her deep-seated anger is expressed through her volcanic eruptions and the lava flows are her tears of frustration and pain bubbling over onto her surface.

Her oceans roar. Her waves roll, sweeping away thousands in her path as she attempts to gain the attention of those who call her their home.

If one were to view The Mother as a gentle, loving Being who has given her all to her children and who is in great distress, due to the actions of some of those children, perhaps then a different picture might emerge.

Unfortunately, both the innocent and the guilty bear the brunt of her anger, her frustration and her deep, deep pain associated with her feelings of betrayal and abandonment.

Her deep-seated feelings are melting her ice-caps and this event is causing her oceans to rise. Oblivious to this event, ones-of-Earth, with greed streaming from their eyes, observe the land beneath the melting snow and they rub their hands together in glee. What great riches lie hidden beneath those rocks that have been covered in deep layers of snow and glaciers of ice for thousands and thousands of decades-of-man's time? They drool in expectation as they ponder on the best methods to explore and exploit these regions.

In despair and desperation, Mother Earth calls upon Father Sky for urgent assistance now.

What form will that assistance take? The call has been heard by the Source-of-All-Life. An answer will be found and delivered. Will it be to humanity's liking? The answer to that question is: probably not.

Appease her anger. Give Gaia hope. Give Earth the love that she craves and deserves. Show her that you care.

Dry her tears of despair. Hear her cry for help. View it for what it is. Super-storms happen for a reason. Earth movements happen for a reason. In this supposedly-enlightened age, can no one see and recognise this fact?

Mother Earth needs your help now. A way has been shown. Direct your Light and your Love to her Heart Centre now. Do so daily and, in the process, raise your own vibratory frequency considerably, as Mother Earth attempts to do so herself, so that she can raise herself above those who seek to destroy her completely.

Leave them gasping in surprise, in awe and in despair as she rises above their clutches. Come along with her for the ride as she changes from a third dimensional planet to a brilliant, shining example of fourth dimensional life – a star on the stage who dances in this universe in Divine Light and Divine Love.

Come with her, beloved of God.

Gaia is on the move. She will wait for no one. Her sleepy, yet loving, children need to rub the sleep from their eyes and to rise with her. A way has been shown clearly. Embrace that planetary healing and come on Home in Love and joy. We await you with arms wide open.

Adieu.

Discourse 5

The Rose

Given the nature of the rose – as a symbol of Love Everlasting – it is surprising then that the rose is not valued more highly than it is on Earth. If this were the case, Love Everlasting would be more highly prized than it is at present.

There is a time of great uncertainty coming and all that will sustain those with peace and hope in their hearts is Love.

During these times, there will be great devastation and much upheaval as an old order is removed and a new transition period arrives. This transition period will not be of a long duration, because a new generation of young ones who will be coming through, will be intent on replacing greed with communal good. They will replace the good of the self with the good of the whole. They will replace apathy with Love.

The symbol for this new generation will be the pink Rose of Love.

The old order will be swept away so suddenly and so swiftly that most heads will be reeling, swamped by the devastation and despair that accompanies these vital and necessary changes on Earth. Free Will – this being the Free Will of the individual – has been permitted for far too long to dominate the entire situation. The catch-cry has been always that 'jobs will be lost and the country's economy will suffer.' Of which country we speak, is irrelevant. The excuse is the same always when greed overrides the good of the community.

The mess, in which The Mother – this being Earth – finds herself now is due to these factors. The pollution of her air, her seas and her lands is beyond what humanity is capable of redressing. Humanity has caused the dilemma. Collectively, humanity is the culprit. Individually, it is the greed of powerful men – as well as a few powerful women – that has brought this situation to the fore at this moment-in-time on Earth. However, they have no solutions to the massive problem, which is of their making and that of their predecessors who lived by the same, overriding principle.

Power and greed replaced peace and Love on Earth long, long ago.

Everything that has occurred on Earth in the Piscean Age was heralded, by those who stood to gain greatly, as being done "in the name of progress". But, progress to what, one must ask. What price 'progress'? If Mother Earth suffers such abominable devastation and destruction – along with the habitat of her beautiful and wild creatures that rely on this same habitat for life-support – then, how does humanity, as a collective force, gain?

There is no gain for anyone or anything in the long-term. However, in the short term, there is massive gain, in a financial sense, for those who perpetrate theses acts of destruction in the name of progress; or, whatever names they choose to use, at the time, to promote their dastardly schemes that serve to assist no one but the promoters.

How much longer will humanity – collectively – choose to turn a blind eye to these piranhas of society? How long before the *good people of Earth* stop their own endeavours, for a sufficient length of time, in order to question these ones, along with their elected leaders who give credence to their abominable schemes?

There will be a new generation who will inhabit Earth. This new generation will start afresh, with a new set of guidelines and a new outlook on life. In truth, it is the age-old way of life-on-Earth. It starts with a deep respect for The Mother who provides the ALL of life. It continues with a reverence for the Earthly Mother that few can recall. At a time when the ones known as The Essenes walked the Earth, such respect and reverence permeated every aspect of daily life.

In this age of so-called *enlightenment* where technology rules ALL, such respect and reverence would cause great peals of laughter to ascend heavenwards should anyone be so insane as to suggest a return to those *idiotic* notions of a bygone age.

If all the technological advances were wiped from Earth in one, swift instant, how would humanity survive? If tomorrow morning, one were to awaken to find that there was no electricity, no water running from the taps, no sewerage system, no transportation and no communication, what would be the reaction of most earth-dwellers?

A mere one-hundred and fifty years ago, most of the above *necessities* did not exist. If one, single rock, hurtling through space, wiped out the satellites and the space station, would any of those *necessities-of-life* that humanity takes for granted now, continue to operate? Yet two centuries ago, these were not even dreamed of in the imagination, with the exception of perhaps a few science-fiction writers. What would have been science-fiction back then is a technological reality now. However, with these technological advances came responsibility – both collectively and at a personal level.

This responsibility was ignored, because the cost, in financial terms, was too great a burden for the greedy promoters of these schemes to countenance. Admittedly, a few brave and forward-thinking ones did attempt to implement ways to protect a fragile planet but, for the most part, these were either ignored or dismantled by ones who came after the *enlightened* ones on the grounds that the schemes were too costly to maintain.

So, Planet Earth has reached the point-of-no-return.

Humanity is incapable of and, for the most part, unwilling to tackle the mess that has been inherited from this and previous generations.

The next generation will be insightful, loving and genuinely concerned about the planet, which it calls *home* and on which many species of wild life and plant-life struggle to exist.

This is the dilemma for Earth now. Compound this situation with a massive planet-wide *war-to-end-all-wars*, which, in all probability, will be religion-based and the problem is enormous.

If the planet is razed-by-fire, due to such a war, few will be left standing at the end of the hostilities. Who is the *victor* is irrelevant.

If the planet is razed-by-fire, due to a series of rocks dropping onto her from above, then God will be blamed.

Either way, the devastation will be the same.

Let us play with *the rock* scenario for a time. This is for the benefit of those whose conscious minds are open, active and functioning now. All others would have turned away before reading beyond page one of this Discourse anyway.

Tomorrow morning, when you awaken, you learn that a large rock has been located out in what is termed *space*. This rock is estimated to be the size of eight football fields. It is unknown, at this stage, if the rock will hit Earth, or just glide by her.

If it hits directly, then everything will shatter from the impact and its aftermath. By *everything* is included the human body and all its internal organs.

So, let us assume that the rock passes by without even a glancing blow. It moves slowly – perhaps taking three days and three nights to pass – and it slides between Earth and the sun. Therefore, the planet is in total darkness for the entire period. The sun's rays cannot reach Earth. So, not only is it very, very dark, but also, it is very, very cold. What now?

The satellites have gone. Therefore, all computer-systems and communication systems are *down*. What is left to be utilised? The water, petrol, gas, sewerage and even car engines are all controlled by computers. Humanity has given its *power away* to a computer-system that is no longer functioning. As a collective-force, humans have no control now. Perhaps, for a short time, old relics might be utilised, but these will run out of petrol or gas in a short space of time. In the nineteenth century, steam-driven engines ruled the world and the waves, but how many of those are in existence still?

In a worst-case scenario, small rocks (perhaps the size of *talents*) might begin falling to Earth at speeds only dreamed of by the drivers of the steam engines. These rocks would be fiery, of course, as they entered Earth's atmosphere. These would cause spot-fires, which would become infernos, in a short space of time. Can we call Fire and Rescue? Of course not, because there is no communication system operating. Besides, there is no way of pumping petrol for the tanks, of operating the engines of the fire trucks, which are computer-generated, and there is no way of pumping water to douse the flames anyway. This is because humanity handed its power over to these great technological dinosaurs of twentieth-century ingenuity. But, the dinosaurs are all extinct now, are they not?

There is one other question that needs to be asked. How was it possible for a prophet of olden times, at the commencement of the Piscean Age, to predict that this would occur? How could he predict that *rocks the size of talents* would fall to Earth? How could he predict that there would be signs in the sun, and in the moon, and in the stars? Was he *seeing* and *knowing* what would occur at the end of the Piscean Age, or early into the Age of Aquarius?

Of course, his words were not listened to or taken seriously by most and he was silenced in the manner that most prophets are silenced always – by the destruction of his physical form.

So, where to from here?

We must come back to The Rose. This is our everlasting symbol of peace and Love. It symbolises everything that all prophets of Divine Love and Divine Light have preached always.

We have, in this Discourse, the whole problem outlined clearly. At the bottom of the scale, we have those who work solely and totally for Self, this being the self-absorbed and self-motivated beings where self-interests override all else.

At the top of the scale, we have ones who work solely and totally for Divine Love and Divine Light, regardless of the personality and the occupation that these ones present to the world as their human persona.

In the middle, we have the majority of Earth's population. These are the *good people of Earth*, regardless of their religion, nationality, skin-tone or gender (including gender-preferences). Their overriding concern is for the safety and welfare of their own family and their friends. Along with this concern is the troubling consequence of out-of-control development, which is destroying the planet. They can see the problem clearly. However, they feel powerless to do anything to resolve it. It is not of their making, but they will be the ones to suffer, along with their children and grandchildren, when the Cause-and-Effect scenario comes into play.

Who are they? They are the silent majority who powerful men and women gamble on the fact that they will remain very silent always. They did so when Hitler rose to power. It is assumed by the powers-that-be that they will do so again.

Unfortunately, there have been times when the silent majority has been whipped into action by unscrupulous and self-serving ones-of-Earth and these have resulted in some very dark times on Earth.

However, on a positive note, the *silent majority* is known by another name. That is: the *good people of Earth*. It is the good people of Earth who must step forward now to lead a lost race of people away from a looming disaster.

How can they do so?

Firstly, by looking beyond the rhetoric of self-serving men and women in every situation and asking, first and foremost, the question: "how does this proposal benefit the planet?"

Secondly, it – the silent majority – must look ahead to a time when all must fall back on his or her own resources in any situation. Everyone must ask the next question: "how can we, as a family (or, as a group) survive for a month or more, without all the basic services that we look to others to provide for us now?"

Thirdly, the good people of Earth need to don a Rose – the symbol of Love Everlasting – and to assist others *in Peace and Love only* to ride out the ensuing storm of upheaval and trauma. A time of cleansing will come. The time-frame is unknown to earth-dwellers. It is for the good people of Earth to look to the future now, so that future generations, along with all who call her Home at this time, can survive and thrive on a rejuvenated planet that is free of the self-serving and self-absorbed ones who have brought Mother Earth to the brink of extinction.

There is no greater endeavour that is more important than this one is now. However, unless all that one sets out to do, in this regard, is done in peace and Love, then it will be all in vain. Adding more dissension and violence to Earth's environment would be counter-productive. There is much too much negativity on her surface now as nation fights nation, race fights race and religion fights religion.

The wise will run from a religion, which is based on hatred of others; walk away from a religion that is based in fear, especially in fear of an Authoritarian God, and embrace a philosophy, or religion, that is based upon the principles of Unconditional Love and Peace to all beings – human and otherwise, including the plant and animal kingdoms.

Recognise and respect the fact that the *Love Energy (Male Aspect) of God* and the *Love Essence (Female Aspect) of God* exist in ALL Creations of the *Loving Father-Mother-God Principle – The Source-of-ALL-Life.*

Energy can change. Energy can transmute. Energy can never, ever be killed or destroyed.

God is Energy. God is Essence. God is The Living, Breathing Fire within us all. God is, also, The Living, Breathing Fire within the planet beneath our feet – the planet that is our life-source!

Respect her. Protect her. Support her. Nurture her. Love her as you would your own mother who gave life to your current physical form. In turn, you will be rewarded one-thousand fold.

Don the Rose of Everlasting, Unconditional Love to show your respect and love for your Earthly Mother and celebrate Mother's Day on every day of the year, in support of Mother Earth who holds you in the palm of her hand, in your fragile state, and who clasps you to her heart.

Whatever you do, do it in Peace and Love always.
May God go with you every step of the way!

Discourse 6

The Suspension Bridge

Having pondered these problems, what is the answer?

Going into deep fear cannot solve anything. This will be a case of lowering one's vibrations to a much lower level. There is a saying that some wise teachers will offer at times. It is: "do not come to me with a problem. Come to me with a solution to the problem and I will tell you if I think it will work."

The obvious answer to the problem of Earth's despair is to assist her to raise her own frequency to a higher level. Then, those who are determined to destroy her (for whatever reason) will need to leave the premises, because they will be unable to stay with her – *vibrationally-speaking*. So, for these ones, keeping Earth down at the low level, at which they vibrate now by their own free will choice, is their best option. How they achieve this goal is irrelevant to them, because they act without compunction and they are in survival mode. Some of these ones are the leaders of countries and nations.

They will not relinquish power under any circumstances. It is not in their personal interest to do so. Therefore, the children of Light will need to step forward and help Mother Earth to rise above their soul-destroying and tight clutches. In doing so, they will be raising their own vibrations greatly, as a consequence. There is a two-fold benefit.

By meeting in small, intimate groups regularly – at least weekly – to bring this great miracle into reality on Earth, would be the ideal method. If all children of Light who are incarnate on the planet now were to meet in such a manner, for this purpose, Mother Earth would be given a wonderful boost in energy. The ones involved would be given a similar boost.

Can you imagine if everyone who was vibrating at the level of the Heart chakra – or, higher still – agreed to meet together in their own special group in their own special place, what would occur? What if they all did so at the one time, regardless of where they were residing physically at that moment-in-time? What if they all agreed to meet at one special place?

There is a special place where we can go together. It is by a stream in a garden beyond Earth where the unicorns roam freely. Let us imagine that we have arrived in this garden and we decide to jump across the gently-flowing stream via the stepping stones, which are positioned in the water. This stream is being fed by a massive waterfall, which is near to the crossing.

Once on the other side, we scramble up the embankment and walk up the slight rise as we traverse a rough but well-worn track. Then, we come to the suspension bridge.

Look across to the coffee shop, which is filled with patrons who are enjoying the carefree, open-air atmosphere. This swaying suspension bridge crosses over a deep ravine that has tall trees growing on the steep embankments on both sides.

What if, on the other side, your special Spirit Guide of Light was waiting and was beckoning to you to venture across this structure? Would you do so?

Let us assume that you were very brave and you did so. Joining with your Guide, you follow him or her up the pathway beyond the coffee shop and you arrive at a massive, white building that you might choose to explore. You may describe it as being similar in design to the famous Taj Mahal of Earth, only gigantic in size.

Here, you can enter the double oak doors, on either the lower or the upper level, and listen to the magnificent voices of the choir in full voice there. Assuming that they are singing the *Eternal Om* and they are doing so without the assistance of any other musical instruments, you would be enjoying a beautiful experience. If this happened to be similar to the music that was playing very quietly – back in the meditation room on Earth – the experience would be enhanced, as well as being extraordinary.

Within the area of the Taj Mahal building now, feel your Guide standing behind you while lifting your hands and arms high in the air.

Breathe deeply. Focus your attention on the point of your own *Diamond-Within* – at the Core Centre of your Being.

Draw down *Divine Light* through your Alpha Point, high above your Crown chakra.

Draw up *Divine Love* from the Core Centre of your Being.

Feel the *Violet Flame* within your own precious *Diamond* ignite.

Imagine that this occurs simultaneously and instantly, just as when a spark ignites a gas flame.

Your *Violet Flame* shoots high up through the centre of your Being, opening and activating all of your chakras simultaneously.

You may see this as a coil, which is similar to the circular stairway inside our lighthouse. If every level within the lighthouse was a representation of our chakra system, the connecting stairway then could be a representation of the spiralling column within all of us. This is known in some languages of Earth as the *Kundilini Column.*

Imagine the *Violet Flame* within you creeping slowly and gently up the spiral of the *Kundilini Column*, just one level at a time as it opens every chakra. As the gentle kiss of the early rays of the morning sun opens the rose bud slowly, see every chakra opening – one step at a time – as the *snake* of *Divine Energy*, combined completely with *Divine Essence*, curls imperceptibly up the spiral within.

Wisdom is needed here, as is a deeper understanding.

To raise Divine (masculine) Energy – as many do – at a very fast rate and without the complete balance of Divine (feminine) Essence can be very dangerous physically. However, when the *Violet Flame* is activated slowly and gently by Divine Light and Divine Love – in accord with Divine Wisdom and Divine Will – *The Pulsing* can be the result.

When activated using Divine Power only, accompanied by the desire of the ego-personality self, working hand-in-hand with the logical, conscious mind, the experience could be negative, in the extreme. As always, it is the *Intent* that counts.

Everything comes back to *Intent and vibratory frequency in all things!*

So, you have crossed bravely over the suspension bridge. You have met with your special Spirit Guide and journeyed to the Taj Mahal on the Astral level. Now, in accord with *Divine Light, Divine Wisdom, Divine Will* and *Divine Love,* you have raised your vibratory frequency and ignited your own special *Violet Flame* within your *Diamond Centre.*

All of your chakras are open and flowing freely. Your Spirit Guide of Light is standing behind you. Your arms are raised high above your head while clasping hands together and forming the letter 'Y'. You are open to receive the full extent of God's Love and God's Light into the depths of your Being, while in a deep meditative state.

Now, through your Heart centre, direct *God's Divine Light* and *God's Divine Love,* through the *Violet Flame,* directly into the Heart Centre of Mother Earth.

With the voices of the choir singing softly while these swirl unceasingly around you, possibly you will experience the *Pulsing.* You feel now that you are *AT-ONE* with your own Special God-Self.

ONENESS is achieved – gently, slowly and easily.

With the moment of release, you request, in accord with your Higher Self, that the Beam of Divine Light and Divine Love be retracted *now.* You draw the Magnificent Beam back into the Core Centre of your Being, to your own precious *Diamond-Within.*

With the conclusion of this wonderful experience, you leave the building. Accompanied by your Spirit Guide, you return to the coffee shop beside the suspension bridge.

At the end of the suspension bridge, you leave your Guide with a fond farewell. Return now to your meditation circle where you come back into the realm of the physical.

In this world where negativity abounds, it is vital to close down your chakras – one at a time, commencing at either the minor chakras of the feet and knees – or, more importantly, with the Base chakra.

Your own Core Centre (your *Diamond-Within*) and your Crown Centre will come back slowly to their own level, in their own time. To close the other centres, just command mentally that these come back – one at a time – to a pinpoint of Light *now*.

Then, command the Crown Centre and the Core Centre to return to their normal size *now*.

You can request that your Higher Self, the Higher Part of you, surrounds you *now*.

If it is felt that extra protection is needed at this time, it is simply a suggestion that, after this exercise has been completed, you can bring a shield of Light over the chakras at the front and another one over the chakras at the back, sealing the shields together with Divine Light. Also, if it feels appropriate, seal these front and back shields with the Cross of THE CHRIST. The shield and the Cross are but optional suggestions for those who wish to avail themselves of an additional cloak of protection. As always, it is a personal choice.

With a group of like-minded, spiritually-aware people meeting together, for the purpose of assisting Mother Earth to raise her vibratory frequency – at the same time as these ones raise their own frequency as a direct consequence – this is of mutual benefit. If a clear quartz crystal were to be positioned in the centre of the meditation circle, it would be possible for everyone to direct his or her individual Beam of Light and Love into the crystal. It is an added benefit to magnify the Beam by whatever (percentage) everyone feels guided to decree personally, before sending a Beam of Unconditional Love Energy and Love Essence, combined with Divine Light, into the Heart of Mother Earth.

It can be magnified ten times or ten thousand times. It is a personal choice. Also, before drifting into meditation, if one were to direct a Beam of Love from the Heart centre to the person who was sitting on the left side in the circle, this act would cause the vibration within the meditation group to rise fast and in a spectacular way, especially if all were participating in this group exercise.

All of the above explanation is a suggestion only. Everyone will find his or her own pathway to understanding and enlightenment.

Just remember that every path, which is walked in Love, is the correct one for you in that moment. It cannot be any other way.

A problem has been highlighted in the Discourse, entitled *The Rose*.

A solution has been given in this Discourse of *The Suspension Bridge*.

Take these suggestions into your heart and, if these *feel* correct for you, adopt them. If another method is more appealing, adopt that one. Free will is a God-given gift. Of course, if you wish, you can choose to use your free will to do nothing at all to assist Mother Earth. She is struggling for survival now as she continues to provide *All* for those seven billion people who are incarnate on her surface. It is a daunting and thankless task.

Try to remember one fact. Mother Earth is a living, breathing Creation of the Father-Mother-God-Principle – The Source of All Life.

Nurture her. Protect her. Return her Love one thousand fold and, if possible, do so weekly, in association with others of like-mind.

In God's Love,
Adieu.

Discourse 7

In All Worlds

In all the worlds, there is but ONE GOD. This is the God of Divine Love and Divine Light.

The planets in this universe, as in all of the other universes, respond to God's Cosmic Law. There is but one planet in this universe that does not comply. The inhabitants of this planet refuse to accept Cosmic Law.

It had been hoped that, given time, they – the inhabitants – would come to this understanding sooner, rather than later.

Unfortunately, this did not occur. There are many ways, in which this could have happened during the past 26,000 years. That is the full cycle of the zodiac as the earth circles the sun. Whether the signs of the zodiac are split into thirteen segments or twelve segments is irrelevant. Two thousand years ago, at the beginning of the Piscean Age, a great Master Teacher came to Earth in physical form.

As the Piscean Age was the last of the zodiacal signs, it was imperative that a great Ascended Master should come to lead the way – once again. His messages were misunderstood by a sleepy population who were under the rule of priests and tyrants. His messages were misconstrued deliberately, in most cases, by ones who saw power in harnessing his words and his works for their own benefit.

With the dawning of Aquarius, it is time for the wise ones of Earth to turn away from all false teachings and to turn their faces back towards the Light – that being the Light and Love of Almighty God.

Is there a God of Power and Might? Who made the sun? Who made the moon? Who made the planet, on which all reside now and whose degradation is almost total now? Did man-of-Earth create these wonders? Or, did they come about simply of their own accord, without Divine Measures?

The children of Light *Know* the answers to these questions. The children who have chosen deliberately darkness over Light will deny the obvious answer. There is one answer only. As God can give, so, too, can God take away. God does not take away, without giving something greater in return. God will give all to the children of Light. For others, all will be withheld until such time as they are prepared to accept Cosmic Law and the consequences that come with that acceptance.

There is but One Law and One Law only. This is the Law-of-One. This is the Law of Divine and Unconditional Love. Through Divine Love, all will be en-*light*-ened. All will come then into the Light and Love of Almighty God.

The God, of Whom I speak, is all powerful and all loving. All children with Love in their hearts can come to the God, of Whom I speak, at any time – day or night – to be healed of pain and sorrow. God awaits all who seek in Love. No one will be turned away.

The ones who have huge karmic debts, which they have refused to repay over many, many lifetimes while incarnate on Earth and elsewhere, are the ones who mislead and misguide our beautiful and loving children of Light. They have a vested interest in doing so. This is because the longer that the planet remains in darkness and the children remain in ignorance, the longer that they can hold off their own personal day-of-reckoning. That is the simple truth of the matter.

Every time that Earth and her inhabitants reach a point where enlightenment is within their grasp and they can rise up – as ONE – to a fourth-dimensional vibratory frequency, thus coming into alignment with all other planets in this solar system where life proceeds in an orderly, peaceful and loving manner, these ones of darkness orchestrate another horror for the inhabitants of Earth to endure. They do so deliberately, callously, cruelly and without a second thought to the horror that they are creating.

Their time has come. In the Piscean Age, they brought about the so-called *witch-hunts*, which were nothing more than the case of the children of Light being led to the slaughter once again. What is termed the *war to end all wars*, followed by a second such scenario a few decades later, can be laid at their doorstep. These catastrophes – man-made, every one of them – were designed to cause the maximum distress, pain, suffering and premature death to many on the planet. Most were the children of Light once again being targeted by these creatures, who have descended so far into darkness that they cannot see the Light anymore.

So, the purpose of this set of Discourses is to open the eyes of those who know that there is a better way, but who do not know how to find that way.

At every point on the grid system of Earth, there is a Being-of-Light who is ready to lead the way. This Being-of-Light may have become a little *sleepy* – spiritually-speaking – while awaiting his or her own spiritual awakening. This is where the one-hundred and forty-four thousand *white knights* are residing. Shortly, they will all *awaken* to an Awareness of their own and, in peace and Love, they will lead others to the Light and Love of Almighty God.

The children of Light are desperate for these leaders to awaken now and to lead the way by example. It will not be done through major media outlets, or in any spectacular way.

It will be done quietly, silently, secretly and in total commitment to the Law-of-One and to the First Cause, Who is God Almighty and All Loving. It cannot be done in any other way.

These will be small, autonomous groups who follow Guidance from within and who are seeking to raise their own vibratory frequency in tune with the planet, our own Earth Mother, and in tune with Cosmic Law and God's Divine Plan for Earth.

This moment of truth can be delayed no longer. The birthing has begun. After Pisces, the Age of Aquarius is the next sign of the zodiac and its arrival marks a new chapter in Earth's history as a new phase of the 26,000 year cycle begins.

So, you see, this is the Divine Plan in action. The Earth is on the move. She cannot be stopped or delayed any longer. Once again, the brave and wonderful children of Light have parachuted in behind enemy lines and they have penetrated the darkness of negativity on the planet with their Divine Light.

So, this is a clarion call to the children of Light to gather together on the energy centres of Earth at the intersecting points of Earth's grid system and to meditate and pray to be shown the way from here. These are the places of safety, to which all Light Workers will be guided. There is a Being of Light awaiting you there. Nowhere else will be safe in the chaos and destruction that is to come as our Earth Mother births herself into fourth-dimensional reality.

It is her birthright, as it is the birthright of all of the children of Light. Come with her. Now is the time to sink into a blissful state of quiet meditation, away from the noise and confusion of the world, and to withdraw and reflect on all that has been revealed to you here and in other publications that have been circulated throughout your world for many decades now.

Come Home in full Consciousness.

Come Home in the Consciousness of THE BUDDHA.

Come Home in the Consciousness of THE CHRIST.

They are one-and-the-same. This is known by another name – *Super-Consciousness*.

The conscious mind needs to be in touch with Super-Consciousness. It is open to ALL. The only drawback to such open communication is the subconscious mind, which is full of learned and erroneous concepts, half-truths and untruths. These have been fed to it, through the conscious mind, since the moment of birth. This happens in every lifetime and in every culture of Earth. In this, we have an example of the divide-and-rule principle working almost to perfection. It is the subconscious mind, which is a sponge that soaks in all information, regardless of its origins, and it does not have the facility to filter, or to discriminate, between what is erroneous and what is truth. This is where the great blockage occurs.

In meditation, we can skip the subconscious mind and go straight to the Source of Super-Consciousness.

These are a few clues to assist the children of Light along the last leg of their journey towards the Light, as they, also, birth themselves into fourth-dimensional reality, along with their Mother – the planet known as *Earth*.

God Speed on your journey. May it be a smooth and wondrous transition for all.

In Peace and Love, I leave you. Goodwill to all.

Discourse 8

The Dawn

A new era has dawned on Earth – a new era that heralds a New Age. The New Age of Aquarius can begin with a whimper of protest, at a spiritual level, as the earth-changes occur. It can begin with a battle of gigantic proportions, after which few will be standing. This is the free-will choice of all who reside on the planet, which is known as *Earth* currently.

This was the choice of those who lived in the time of Noah. Unfortunately, they chose the battle option. While the majority of Earth's population was fighting amongst itself – fuelled by the hatred being dispensed by the rulers of the day (tyrants, one-and-all), as well as by the priests of the various religious sects that were permitted to flourish under the auspices of those tyrannical rulers – others were being guided from Within.

Those who listened to and followed their own innate Inner Guidance were busy building boats. Noah's Ark is symbolic. Many such vessels were constructed. Many children of Light escaped the carnage and destruction. The final outcome was that Earth was cleansed completely and all who had sought to destroy their beautiful Earthly Mother – their home away from Home – were removed and were required to account for their actions.

Unfortunately, many, many children of Light perished with them, as they were caught up in the battle and its aftermath.

Unfortunately, we have *come-full-circle* with the closing of the Age of Pisces. The last great battle did not conclude, because neither side had time to strike the last fatal blow before the floods came.

Unfortunately, the self-same men and women are in control again now. The same tyrants have set up their power-bases in places where they are *big fish* in small ponds. United, they will be a powerful force to defeat. When the last great battle begins – with ideology at its base – there will be no end once again. A similar scenario will occur, in all probability, but the cleansing will not come by water. Another method will be utilised.

The children of Light, who can see a similar scenario unfolding before their eyes, will be guided to places of safety, as they were in a previous time. Others will have no alternative but to accept the fate that befalls them in the final hour of Earth's great upheaval. The birth-pangs commenced many decades ago, as our children of Light recognised back then. These have gone on unabated until the present moment.

The speeding up of what is known as *Time* is the greatest clue as the beautiful Earth Mother raises her vibratory frequency, in accord with Cosmic Law. This is the reason for the natural disasters that are occurring with surprising frequency now. This is why the rulers-of-the-day have no answers for their people. There are no answers. Everything has moved beyond the control of those who are incarnate on the planet now.

The moment of birth approaches rapidly. No battle on Earth – great or small – can prevent its arrival. The birth, of which I speak, is of a spiritual nature as Mother Earth shakes off the shackles of third-dimensional imprisonment and she rises in all her glory – as a bride on her wedding day – to fourth-dimensional reality.

Who is coming with her, at her moment of *Awakening* into the dawn of spiritual enlightenment? It will be those who can *see* what is occurring on Earth and who are powerless to prevent the looming disaster.

Unfortunately, once commenced, the tidal wave cannot be stopped. It is a tidal wave of negativity, which has increased to gigantic proportions – as it did in that previous Age, of which I spoke earlier.

What is to be done? All that can be done now is for the wise ones to lift the scales of misunderstanding from their sleepy eyes and to listen, with the ears of Spirit, to Inner Guidance. As a bride on her wedding day then, raise the vibratory frequency – through a deep, meditative state-of-being – and rise up with your Earth Mother in full glory and full awareness.

It is oh-so-simple. To become caught up in the upheavals and the battles would be unhelpful in the extreme.

The lamps of the bodies – these being the chakra centres – will need to be clear and flowing freely for the Guidance to come. That is the secret.

To become caught up in all that is created deliberately by the tyrants and their sycophantic priests will cause nothing but fear and negativity. This will spread as a cancer does. This will cause the energy centres of the body to slow down or to spin in reverse. This is counter-productive, because there can be no Guidance received by anyone who is in this state. Only in a deep, meditative state as one seeks to commune with the God Within, can strong Guidance be received by the seeker.

Unfortunately, this is not the way of Earth. The wise will heed the message and meditate daily. The unwise will believe that the world can go on as it is indefinitely. So, where does the answer rest? It is hidden deep within everyone on the planet now. Some of the children born of Light will listen. It is to these beautiful ones that these messages are directed.

Meditate daily to receive Inner Guidance. Follow Inner Guidance to the letter and you will be where you are meant to be when all around you descends into chaos. Follow the conscious, rational, logical mind that controls the ego-personality self and you will be left to your own devices. You will need to make your own arrangements for your personal safety and that of your loved ones. I repeat – Earth and her inhabitants have *come-full-circle!*

The dying days of Pisces have brought nothing but chaos. Take up arms against one another and the end will come sooner rather than later.

Only those who live in Love and who live a simple life based on Love – as shown by the leader-of-all-leaders who came at the beginning of the Age of Pisces – will be permitted to remain on Earth.

All others will be required to leave all and to vacate the premises forthwith.

These are the two options and they are the only two options open to all.

The loving children of Light must lead the way.

The loving children of Light must meditate daily in order to know the way.

Only then can they lead others to a better – and a more Loving – way of life.

This is my message to the world.

Walk only in Love.

Walk only in Light.

Walk in the Love and Light of our Divine Father-Mother-God-Principle – the Source of All Divine Love and Divine Light.

Peace on Earth. Goodwill to All.

Discourse 9

The Garden

(From the fifth book of the Series, ***ERROR PROFOUND***)

There is a garden. This garden is a very special place. It is a place of peace, of quiet and of reflection.

In this garden, many people live in serenity and tranquillity. Where is this garden? It is only a thought away.

Come into my magical garden for a short while. Forget the cares of your chaotic world of physical life. Come!

There are tall trees whose fingers reach up to touch Father Sky. There are bushes with fruits of various shapes and sizes drooping from the branches. There are vines with other fruits and these are hanging over trellis-type structures. In my garden, there are brightly-coloured flowers whose faces are turned towards the sun in the sky. Colourful birds flit from branch to branch, singing their own special songs of praise to the Creator-of-All in thanks for all that has been provided for their joy, their pleasure and their sustenance, in the form of Love, on a daily basis.

If the Creator-of-All would provide for the birds and the animals of the garden, would He/She not provide all for the ones, who choose – of their own free will – to reside in this garden of beauty and wonder? It is truly so.

How does one reach the garden? It is through meditation, of course. Allow me to take you there and to a special grotto within the garden. This is your place alone. No one else can or will come here.

It is a rock formation that is positioned by a gently-flowing stream. Beneath this rock enclosure, which sits on a slight rise, you can see the garden in its entirety. The stream gurgles over smooth river rocks beneath you. The birds flit from branch to branch while singing their sweet songs of joy. Fish jump in the stream. Small animals scurry about as they perform their daily chores associated with the raising of their families. In parts, there are hives of activity. In other areas, the serenity is soul-soothing.

So, let us sit for a time in our grotto, being the passive, silent observer. A lion walks slowly by and he is followed by a white tigress, with several cubs in tow. There is no fear here. No one needs to hunt or to kill. All is provided. The garden is resonating to a fourth dimensional frequency, so no one is in physical form. It is only the physical form that requires food, shelter, rest and sleep. At the higher frequency levels, no such necessities are required.

Our grotto is cool and inviting as we relax on a flat rock while watching the world go by us at a steady pace. I use the term, '*we*', because you have been joined by your own special Spirit Guide now. Your own, very special Higher Self, who is the Higher Part of you, descends as a soft cloud around you, surrounding you in protection and Love. This is, of course, Divine Love, in which you float now.

Stay awhile. Relax in the Now-Moment here, in this special place. Close your eyes. Hear the sounds. Smell the roses on the nearby bushes. Sense the rays of the sun as these permeate all. Feel the Love Essence of your Higher Self surrounding you now.

If necessary, ask a question that is troubling you in your 'other' world, that being the world of the physical. Make the question short, concise and clear. If the answer does not come immediately, it may be waiting for you when you awaken in your own bed on the next morning. Try not to become emotional over the issue that is troubling you, because this may cause you to leave your garden sanctuary abruptly. This is due to the fact that the emotional response has lowered your vibratory frequency, so that you will find yourself back in physical form very rapidly. Then, you will be required to go on with your day's activities there and your special place in your special garden recedes in your consciousness.

That is all that happens. Your special garden is always there, awaiting your return. It is but a thought away. When the cares and dramas of the world are too much to bear, there is no need to turn to alcohol, drugs or another type of stimulus in the form of computer games or sporting activities. All you need to do is to remove all forms of distraction, such as television sets, telephones and people – both large and small – who might be expected to invade "your space" while you are away visiting your garden, in association with and surrounded by your own precious and ever-present Higher Self.

Come to the grotto, dear ones. Come to the Garden of Love.

In God's Light, you will find your way there.

Adieu.

Discourse 10

The Leaning Tower

L et us return to our peaceful garden and to sit for awhile beside our rock formation by the gently-flowing stream. Relaxing on the flat, smooth river rock, we can place our feet into the cool, refreshing water while allowing it to lap our ankles with its soothing caress.

While so engaged, look down to the right section of the garden. In the lower section there, you will see a mist. It is almost as though a dark cloud has descended over that lower level of our garden.

We are perfectly safe on our rock. However now, we become the observers as we peer through the murky mist. What can we see there?

There is a circular structure, which is a very tall tower. It is built of dark brick and, to a degree, it resembles a lighthouse. But, this tower is far from the ocean. It does have a glass dome on top. This is made of a very dark glass – almost black – so very little light or sunlight penetrates its interior.

On the ground level, there is an exceedingly wide verandah, with a covered roof and lattice protecting its side structure. There are wide stairs, of one or two steps, and these lead into our garden. At the bottom of these steps, there is a garden path that is not wide – possibly one would need to traverse this path in single-file. This pathway, at the bottom of our garden, leads to a fence. It is a very high stone structure with a single gate, which appears to be locked.

Let us study the ones who live on the verandah for a short while. They are busy with their daily life activities. Life here was slow and peaceful once. Now, it is endured at a fast, furious, even frantic pace. The inhabitants work hard and they work even harder as they force themselves to play hard.

The faster that they work and play, the more tired and stressed they become. They reach for stimulants, in the form of coffee, tea, alcohol and even drugs, in order to survive to endure another day of their chosen verandah life.

They do not know that we are observing them. How could they? In their semi-dark world, they do not even bother to peer through the lattice, because if they do, they might see the beautiful garden. In fact, they use ridicule often to denigrate those who insist that the garden really does exist. We know it exists, because we are sitting here, enjoying the peace and tranquillity as we commune with nature. In the reality of the verandah, this other reality of peace and Love does not exist. In order to survive financially, these verandah-dwellers must work to earn their keep and to justify their own existence to all who reside there with them. It is a sad situation.

So, for whom do these verandah-dwellers work?

It is for the privileged ones who choose to reside inside the tower. They make the rules and these are enforced rigidly. By whom are these rules enforced? It is by the heavy-handed ones who reside on the ground floor of the tower.

This tower, by the way, is leaning. It resembles the leaning tower of Pisa, in Italy. There are cracks on its outer walls, but few have noticed as yet. Only by sitting at our vantage point in the supposedly non-existent garden can one view the extent of the damage. It is worse than anyone imagines and the cracks that have appeared have placed some considerable strain on the glass dome at the top.

Inside, there are six mezzanine floors (or levels). Every one of the levels is divided into six sections. The *foot-soldiers,* who carry out the directives of their commanders to the letter, live on the ground floor. These foot-soldiers give absolute allegiance to their commanders who they aspire to emulate – and possibly to replace. It is the foot-soldiers who employ the verandah-dwellers. Some verandah-dwellers aspire to emulate – and possibly to replace – the ones in command on the ground floor. So, there is a definite and well-defined pecking-order in place in the lower level of the garden. However, the mist and dark cloud rarely lift so, unless one peers closely and studies the leaning tower carefully, its inhabitants and their futile endeavours would pass unnoticed.

The six levels on those mezzanine floors represent the financial section, religious section, educational section, military section, communication (media) section and the scientific/medical section.

Within every level, there are six definite sub-sections and these are fiercely competitive – all vying for superiority.

The whole interior is a very dark place to live, work and play. However, the ones who choose to reside here do not notice, because they have become accustomed to the darkness. Their eyes and their senses (those that are functioning still, that is) have adjusted to the semi-darkness of the tower's interior. So absorbed are they in the silly games that they play – all day and all night – they do not even realise that there is an outer verandah attached to the tower, which has developed a spectacular lean to it in recent times.

Will it collapse, do you think? It must do so, unless urgent steps are taken to repair the structure. But, if the commanders cannot see that there is a problem in the first place, then how can they begin to fix it?

The verandah-dwellers – or, those ones whose consciousness is not quite so dull – have noticed, but they are not taken seriously when they mention this fact. Besides, they do not wish to *rock any boats*. After all, their own livelihood and the needs of their immediate family members must take precedence over all else. The commanders must know the problem is there, they reason within themselves, because they are the controllers-of-all in the lower garden where the tower is situated.

If we were to equate the verandah-dwellers with the *Good People of Earth*, at what frequency would they be functioning?

Most would be at the level of the Solar Plexus chakra, with a few more enlightened souls vibrating at the level of the Heart chakra. All of their Higher chakras would be blocked, or perhaps spinning in reverse.

What of the ones inside the leaning structure? These are the ones who control all, so they operate at the vibratory frequency of the Sacral chakra – the point of Divine Power, which they misuse daily and nightly. They occupy the six upper levels and they continue to cause friction within those levels, which they have been allotted.

The ones on the ground floor are the ones who are base in nature. They operate at the level of the Base or Root chakra. These ones have no conscience, no morals and no compunction whatsoever when it comes to carrying out the orders of their commanders – and to the letter, if not beyond it. The tyrannical armies, the paedophiles and murderers come into this category.

Those who continue to drift out into the garden regularly are the ones who have great difficulty breathing on the verandah, so their visits to the garden become more frequent and their times spent on the verandah are those that are dictated by necessity now. These ones would be the spiritual beings who vibrate at the level of the Heart chakra (at a minimum), or at the Throat and Third Eye chakras.

The Heart chakra is Divine Love; the Throat chakra is Divine Will; The Third Eye chakra is Divine Wisdom/Mind while the Crown Point is Divine Light (illumination/ideas).

To the ones who vibrate at the upper level of the vibratory scale, the destruction of the tower is inevitable. It is on borrowed time as the lean becomes more pronounced and the cracks in its structure become longer and deeper. The ones within its walls face imminent annihilation, but they cannot see this fact. They believe that their *house-of-cards*, which they constructed long, long ago, can go on forever.

It is the ones on the verandah who have the choices to make. They can look up, acknowledge the cracks, run down the verandah stairs, jump the path and rush to the safety of the garden of Love and Light. Or, alternatively, they can run inside and call upon the commanders of the tower for protection.

Why must they jump the path? The path leads to the garden fence, with the single gate. The single gate opens one-way only. There is no way to return to the tower once one passes through the gate.

However, to the observers who sit on the rock in the garden, this whole elaborate stage play is all illusion anyway. The tower will fall. It was erected by man, assisted by woman. The glass dome will explode. The stone walls will crumble. The verandah will be torn asunder. The rubble will turn to dust and the grass and vines will grow over the unsightly mess.

But, what of its seven billion inhabitants who dwell there? They will be traumatised for a long, long time. They have played the *games-of-Earth* for so long that most do not acknowledge or accept any other way of life, or any other form of existence. They will turn around eventually – and, of their own accord, in their own time – and be dazzled by the sight of the beautiful, enchanting garden that was waiting there for them and their enjoyment and their pleasure for life everlasting. Truly, then will they be able to say – in truth and sincerity –

"I AM in this world, but I AM not of it!"

Discourse 11

Silver Linings

Clouds with silver linings have a precious diamond-within. What is within is being hidden from view temporarily. Perhaps, the hidden treasure is the moon goddess whose silver rays stream forth as these play hide-and-seek with the silent observer.

Perhaps, that which is hidden behind other clouds is the golden ball, known as the sun-god in some cultures. One is the feminine essence – a soft, gentle glow. One is the masculine energy – an action-taking hero. When the essence and the energy are combined AS-ONE, miracles occur. The first miracle would be that the cloud hiding their union would dissipate instantly, due to the combined Love Energy and Essence of the two who are pervading it.

There are seven billion *clouds* on the planet at present. Some are stormy and aggressive. Others are stationary and lost. Floating amongst these ones are others that are light and fluffy. The stormy ones are seeking their love essence that they abandoned somewhere many millennia ago. Others are seeking their long-lost energy, without which they cannot function for any length of time. The light and fluffy clouds are intact, but they need to hide their great Light and their great Love behind a wall of normalcy in order to survive.

The light and fluffy clouds need to bring their own energy and essence into Perfect Balance. With the soul-spirit that is within these ones, the equation may be a 60% - 40% mix. When these ones remove their cloudy masks and show themselves in their full glory, the ones who are attuned to the moon goddess – the Silver Ray – only, will realise that there is another way to live one's life. They will look for answers persistently while searching for a way to be as bright and as clear as their counter-parts who were *cloudy* once, also.

The stormy clouds will huff-and-puff while claiming that there is no other way, but their way. However, they will not be able to remain anywhere near the Light Ones now, because The Light will begin to melt their rough and gruff exterior and they will be in danger of dissipating all of that stormy exterior.

Until these ones come into Perfect Balance with the other part of themselves – their feminine essence and moon goddess – they will continue on with their aggression and their silly war-games that have brought the planet to the brink of extinction. They will find that using God's Will as an excuse for their atrocious and soul-destroying behaviour will not be sufficient to save them from their eventual demise.

A sun-god entity, without the balance of the moon goddess essence, is a cloud on the brink of self-annihilation. Finding a moon goddess cloud who is similarly handicapped will alleviate the problem temporarily.

The moon goddess cloud will be compliant, obedient, subservient and loving. The two separate clouds can come together for a short time only. After that, the storm cloud of masculine energy will devour and destroy the cloud of feminine essence, because the sun-god must control always. He is required then to seek another moon goddess cloud, for he needs her essence to survive. He has misplaced his own Divine Essence long, long ago.

What caused these clouds to relinquish the other part of themselves?

It was the birth of ego!

The Gold Ray of God and the Silver Ray of God must be merged completely, totally and in Perfect Balance – as God is Perfect Balance – for the cloud to disappear and for the True Being of Light and Love to shine forth for all to see and to appreciate the Glory of God in embodiment on Earth.

Then, and only then, can the brilliant Diamond-Centre within all of God's Creations – on Earth and elsewhere – be seen in Its True Light.

Light will engulf the planet as Love works Its Miracles daily.

Peace on Earth. Goodwill to All.

Discourse 12

With Eyes Wide Open

With eyes wide open, reside with me in the garden where Divine Light and Divine Love permeate all.

What is the most pressing need for the observers in our garden at the moment? It is to bring an *Awareness* to the ones who choose to reside on the verandah. Awakening these loving souls to *Awareness* is crucial now. As has been stated previously, the verandah-dwellers represent the *Good People of Earth*. These are the only ones who can be rescued now from the folly that has been caused and perpetrated by the ones known as the *Tower Dwellers*. For the ones who choose to live in the negative, lower state inside the Tower, it is too late to negotiate a reprieve. Their Akashic Records are open to the scrutiny of all now.

For those on the verandah, a period of Grace has been offered. If these ones allow fear to assail them, they will run inside the Tower seeking protection from the negative masters who rule there. That protection will be given, but there will be a very high price to pay.

Absolute allegiance to the negative cause will be demanded.

For those who choose to step out in faith and Love, just one more time, the steps to the garden are open. However, this is a daunting step to take. These ones do all in their power to convince themselves and their loved ones that the verandah is as safe as it has been always. They use this mantra daily to delude themselves into believing that life can and will go on as it has done always on the verandah.

What needs to occur now is for the garden-dwellers, as well as the garden-observers who visit there on a regular basis, to start to speak out – softly, gently and in Divine Love. The verandah-dwellers need to be coaxed down those two, wide steps to the garden. They need to be persuaded that all is safe there. They need to be shown that it is necessary to jump the path, which leads to the one-way gate that is narrow and heavy.

Those who have *Awakened to Awareness* already can be silent no more. The verandah-dwellers are frightened. They are bombarded day and night by negativity. Negativity is a cancer – the cancer of fear.

Gently, unobtrusively and slowly, the Awakened Ones need to step out in faith and Divine Love now. They must reach up – ever-so-slowly – and they must remove the outer, lattice wall, which prevents the verandah-dwellers from peering into the garden. In so doing, the Awakened Ones will allow the Divine Light that permeates the entire garden to flood the verandah.

One of two events will happen. Those in fear and negativity will run as fast as they can into the interior of the leaning tower while believing this to be the safest place there is. In so doing, they are sealing their own fate by rejecting outright the Divine Grace that is being offered temporarily to those who reside on the verandah.

Others will stand transfixed on the verandah and they will be astounded by the fact that the garden has been there all the time and they did not know of its existence. For a time, they will experience anger and this will be directed towards the six leaders of the six levels that control the six factions within every level. Eventually, the Awakening Ones, whose Awareness is opening further and rapidly, will come to the acceptance that the leaders and their blind followers did not know of the existence of the garden of Divine Light and Divine Love. They did not know, because for lifetime-after-lifetime-after-lifetime in their dark, negative world, they have shunned the Light and the Love of God – our Creator-of-All.

Some of them may have dressed in fancy robes and convinced themselves that they were leading a *religious* life, as a way of leading their followers along a parallel path. However, there is a grave and great difference between leading a *religious* life and of leading a *spiritual* life. The Awakened, Enlightened Ones will *Know* the difference. All others will assume that these two states are one and the same.

It is possible to be religious without being spiritual. It is possible to be both at the same time and many of our verandah-dwellers fall into this category. It is possible to be spiritual without following the religious dogma, doctrine and directives of a particular and/or popular creed.

Our Awakened garden-dwellers fall into this category. There are some who reside, for the most part, in the garden while donning robes of a particular religion. But, this is more for the benefit of those on the verandah who the monks – for want of a better description – are attempting to coax – one step at a time – down the stairs and out into the garden of Light and Love.

It is all a question of consciousness, rather than a question of dress choice. The ones in the interior of the Tower are living a life of living hell, but it is all that they know, so they do not realise or accept this fact. The ones on the ground floor vibrate at the frequency of Divine Life – there is no level lower than that one. Their masters, on the upper levels of the mezzanine floors, vibrate at the level of Divine Power, the misuse of which creates great karmic debt.

The ones who reside on the verandah, but who are in-tune with the masters inside the Tower and who jump to their tune constantly, are vibrating at the level of Divine Order, the chakra of Balance. These ones can jump either way. They can lower their frequency to that of Divine Life and/or Divine Power; in so doing, they are contravening Cosmic Law. There is a high price to pay when this is the choice that is made.

The remaining verandah-dwellers are frozen in fear. They vibrate at a frequency that is fluctuating between Divine Order and Divine Love. Some are *Awakening to Awareness*. Others are too frightened to do so. The difference between the two is that one operates on logical, conscious thought to the exclusion of all else – as at the Divine Order level. The other vibrates to the frequency of Divine Love more often than at that of Divine Order, so they follow their intuitive, inner guidance more often than they follow logical, conscious thought. These are the ones who will need to take the brave step of stepping down onto the stairs that lead to the garden.

The Awakened Ones who are standing ready to assist, are shaking their heads in amazement as they watch many, many of the verandah-dwellers removing the well-entrenched values that are being discarded and the firmly-stuck scales that are being removed from the eyes of these beautiful ones. Slowly, tentatively and in trepidation, they are moving bravely towards the first step down into our beautiful garden of Divine Light and Divine Love.

The illusion of the Tower has been shattered. They cannot believe now that they were so blind that they could not see. Soon, all that will be left will be the garden anyway. Those who are steeped in the third-dimensional illusion of the Tower and all that it stands for will be lost for a long, long time, once the Tower and its accompanying structure disintegrates. That is all that can happen from here. The negativity of its inhabitants has assured its demise.

If we were to be so bold as to equate the Tower with life-on-Earth at present and to acknowledge the illusion of it all, what would that tell us about the state-of-play at the moment?

Civilisations on Earth have come and gone. For the most part, they simply self-destruct when the negativity becomes too great for the individual soul-spirit to survive. Earth has reached the point-of-no-return in its experiment with third-dimensional reality.

It is time to return to *the Garden!*

The garden vibrates at a fourth-dimensional frequency. Outside our garden – and beyond the illusionary fence, with the one-way gate – there is another garden that would blind those of a lower frequency with its brilliance. This is the level of the fifth dimension. It has been stated many times that these other dimensions exist and that within all three dimensions, there are seven levels of consciousness. At the Highest Level – beyond the seventh level of Consciousness of the fifth dimension – there is the One Who is Higher Still. The Loving Mother-Father-God-Principle is at the Level of the Highest Frequency of all – the Twenty-Second Level.

If this statement written above is correct, this would make the level of those on Earth – who rule within our illusionary Tower – of a very retarded consciousness indeed.

The Tower has cracks that are deepening daily. Mother Earth has cracks that are deepening daily. The ones in the garden of Light and Love can see this fact very clearly. Will the ones on the verandah wake up before it is too late to abandon the verandah and jump for the safety of the garden?

This is the question that everyone will need to ask of him or her-self very soon, because life on Earth – in its present form – cannot go on the way it has been proceeding for very much longer. The reason is simple. The planet cannot take the strain for much longer. She cannot take the strain of seven billion people polluting her and desecrating her daily and nightly. Mother Earth is a living breathing Creation of the Mother-Father-God-Principle. In her own right, she is a beauteous creation.

In her current form, *Mother Earth is convulsing!*

Earth is raising her vibratory frequency to a fourth dimensional level. She is in dire need of assistance to do so.

Those who cannot rise with her will be required to vacate the premises in a short time. They will need to be in a transitory state until they can accept the finality of what has occurred.

Those who do make it out to the garden of Divine Light and Divine Love will be joined by others who are vibrating at an even higher frequency – those from the fifth-dimensional realm – because much healing will be required for those who survive the trauma and who will need to re-group as they commence life again on a pristine planet.

All will be capable of doing so, because they will be hampered no longer by the ones with the retarded consciousness who held everyone in their sway for oh-so-long.

All will possess an expanded consciousness then as they observe, in wonder and amazement, the reconnection between *Father Sky* and *Mother Earth*. The entire cosmos will stand still when that day dawns. This is a rare sight indeed. It is one that Mother Earth has fought valiantly and persistently to achieve for a long, long time.

Without the great assistance provided to her by the children-of-Light who have continued to incarnate upon her, despite their great suffering in lifetime after lifetime, it would have been a feat that was close to impossible.

It is the children-of-Light who need to turn this world around now – through Divine Light and Divine Love. To do so in any other manner would be to play into the hands of the negative ones who rule her at present. By playing the games-of-Earth that the negative ones with the retarded consciousness promote, would be counter-productive. Through dissension, or at the point of a gun, is not the way of Light.

The Way-of-Light is to draw down the Divine Light of God from the Alpha Point above one's head and to draw up the Divine Love of God from the Core Point within one's own Centre. To do so either alone or in a group setting – in silence and serenity – will achieve a far more positive and loving outcome in the long term.

The more Light Beings involved, the greater the impact, of course.

When all chakras are open and flowing freely, it is time to utilise the brilliant Beam of Light that has been generated and drawn down through the Alpha Point as Divine Love is drawn up from the Core Centre – our Diamond Within. Then, we can pour Divine Light and Divine Love from our Heart centre directly into the Heart centre of Mother Earth.

In no time at all, her Ascension-into-Light will occur. *With eyes wide open*, all will be astounded. This ascent is a spectacular sight to witness in any reality. History may record the following statement:

Of the seven billion people who were incarnate on Earth – just prior to her magnificent transition – most were the children-of-Light who fought the cancer of fear and negativity to the end.

Mother Earth – the Jewel in the Crown of this Universe – with her transition to fourth-dimensional frequency, is a "Star" to behold!

Truly, a "Star" is born!

Discourse 13

Reincarnation and Karmic Consequence

As gentle as a mountain breeze, the mist of ignorance does lift. Once Truth is revealed, secrets held sacred by but a few are released in Love Everlasting.

There comes a time when all must open hearts and minds to a new and different Reality. This can happen slowly as the dawn's rays open the rose bud to the brilliance of new life. It can happen suddenly and dramatically as when a storm arises seemingly from nowhere and lightning flashes pierce the darkness just before the breaking of the gentle dawn.

Either way, the effect is the same. Awakening occurs. The *Awakening to Awareness* is upon humanity now. The dawn can be delayed no longer. It was hoped that humanity would open its eyes ever so slowly and ever so gently midway through the Age of Pisces when the little ones of God's Light came in Love to lift the veil.

God's children of Pure Love came in droves to Earth. They were full of joy, hope and Love while wearing the mantle of Truth upon their shoulders.

Their fate was sealed from the moment of their birth. Everyone was marked for destruction by a force so powerful that Mother Earth is in deep despair still as it holds her in its clutches. That force is the cancer of negativity, which is fuelled by false teachings and erroneous beliefs.

If there is only one lifetime on Earth for everyone, this belief then places great power in the hands of a few as they seek to control and to govern through fear.

When our precious ones came down to the darkness of a negative planet – midway through the Age of Pisces – they were led to the funeral pyre while alive still. Their captors, tormentors and the demented mob that these ones had roused to a fevered state, shouted for blood. This terrible tragedy occurred, because a frightened humanity did not wish to awaken gently to an *Awakened State of Awareness*. True Reality beckoned then. Ignorance prevailed.

These children of Light – the precious ones who were slaughtered in their thousands world-wide – are waiting in the wings to descend to Earth again. As before, they hope to bring forth a new Consciousness – as did THE CHRIST – as did THE BUDDHA.

It is the same consciousness. This is the consciousness of Divine Love. Divine Love is all-pervading. Divine Love is all-knowing. Divine Love is unconditional. Divine Love is being without guile. Divine Love is all encompassing and non-judgemental. Divine Love is the birthright of all. These children of Love know no other state but this state of Grace, buoyed by Divine Love and protected by Divine Light.

In the face of Divine Love and pierced by Divine Light, negativity retreats. There is nothing that sends a person who is steeped in negativity into fear more quickly than the vision of a child-of-Light coming towards the physical form of that person who is in embodiment.

These negative ones do not understand, at a conscious level, why they should feel this way about another person who is in embodiment in the physical world at the same time as they are walking the Earth. Their instinctive reaction is the same always. They attack.

This attack may be verbal. It might be subtle and underhand. It may be violent and physical. Always, it is unprovoked and unexpected. The little one who works solely in God's Love and Light cannot understand why an unprovoked attack of this nature should occur.

The answer is simple. The one in negativity reacts in fear. It is a fear born of dread. The dread stems from the fact that one day, he or she will be forced to face the Light. The Light of Truth will dawn on Earth and the negative ones who control all on Earth will be forced to face their moment-of-truth. A hand will be upon the shoulder of the one in fear and negativity and his or her Akashic Records will be opened for all the ones of Earth and elsewhere to witness.

The deeds of past encounters and past lives will be there for all to see as the perpetrator is faced with his or her horrendous acts. There will be much pleading. There will be much denial. There will be blame placed elsewhere on others, because the ones facing-up to past deeds will never accept blame or guilt. Everything that has occurred in horrendous times of slaughter and upheaval on Earth has been the fault of someone else always.

So, an impasse has been reached. The ones in negativity do not want to bring about the Intervention of the Light-of-Understanding too soon on Earth. In their hearts, they know that the day-of-reckoning must come for them and for their fellow-travellers on the *negative pathway*. They live in fear. They act accordingly.

Their current actions are having a devastating effect on our Earthly Mother. Worse is yet to come at their hands unless, of course, Divine Intervention comes sooner rather than later. These ones, of whom I speak, are steeped in negativity and they will stop at nothing to hold onto all that they have gained. They are walking a tight rope, because they do not want to tip the scales in the favour of THE LIGHT. This is their greatest fear. At present, they are tolerating those whose Consciousness has opened and who have arisen to an *Awakened State*. They tolerate them, because they do not want to bring on a war that would be so devastating that few will survive.

Before the invention of weapons of mass destruction, they would do so, in the blink of an eye, and they would have had no compunction in sending the sons of the children of Light off to fight those wars with devastating consequences for the families concerned. They, of course, would hide behind the facade of being in control – from a distance.

What do you think will be the reaction of these monsters-of-negativity when our beautiful children of God's Light and Love begin to descend to Earth, via the birth process, shortly? Their arrival is imminent. Their arrival cannot be stopped or delayed. Their arrival will tip the balance drastically – in favour of Love Everlasting and Light untrammelled.

At the time of Jesus, they – the negative ones – orchestrated the destruction of the physical bodies of all male babies under the age of two years. This was not just to eradicate a future CHRIST from their midst. This was to rid the planet of his supporters who were coming to assist in his great mission of opening the eyes of a sleepy humanity to a Higher Consciousness and to Unbounded Light, as well as to Love Divine.

History has recorded that story as history has recorded the tragedy of the witch-hunts half-an-Age later. Now, with the dawning of the new Age of Aquarius, we have a new beginning for all who reside on Earth.

The residents of this slowly-dying planet can choose to act. They can choose to follow the dictates of these monsters who live in the darkness of negativity and who control all media outlets, which will spread their message of fear and hatred widely.

The residents of Earth can choose to turn a blind eye once again as they look to their own safety and protection. They can, once again, choose to do nothing to prevent the excesses of the negative ones who seek to control at all costs.

The inhabitants of Earth can, if they so choose, lift the veil of ignorance from their very sleepy eyes and wake up to what is occurring around them.

Now, it is the *Good People of Earth* who must choose to act in Love, to walk unaided in the Light and to embrace the philosophy and the Love of the children of Light as they descend one-by-one into Earth's negativity. Truly, they are coming to assist a sleepy population to raise its vibratory frequency – at an individual level – so that the majority of Earth's population can rise up with their Mother as she breaks free of the clutches of the soul-destroying negativity that permeates every fibre of her being.

Make no mistake. These new, little ones – come fresh to the planet – are the cavalry who are parachuting in behind enemy lines!

This is a great and brave sacrifice on their part. They have no reason to come otherwise. They are without guile or guilt. They are loving and beautiful examples of the Divine Love Principle in Perfect Action.

Let their great sacrifices of yesteryear be not in vain.

THE CHRIST means Divine Love and THE CHRIST means Divine Light. At a personal level, THE CHRIST is within all of us. No one is exempt. All can choose to crush THE CHRIST within – as the negative ones do. All can choose to ignore – as many people do now. No one can deny the Presence of THE CHRIST WITHIN.

When the great saviour, Jesus, came, he was born a Jewish boy who was named *J'shua,* the son of Joseph and of Mary. His name was not *Jesus Christ.* He became THE CHRIST through a life of purity and of Divine Love.

In many parts of the world, his birth is celebrated once a year. People, with Love in their hearts, come together and they sing great songs of praise in remembrance of his birth, his life and his subsequent death at the hands of the evil ones, who rule the planet to this day.

The creatures-of-darkness, of whom I speak, come to Earth in different guises, different bodies, different cultures and religions, but their lives are lived in and filled with negativity always. They have the one, over-riding principle. That is *Control or Destroy.*

So, has THE CHRIST of the Aquarian Age descended to Earth now, in a new physical form?

One of the greatest supporters of the one known as *Jesus of Nazareth* was his beloved disciple who has come to be known as *John, the Beloved.* It was John who is reported to have recorded the prophecies of REVELATION in THE BIBLE. It was predicted that he would be needed to record prophecy again. Did the great Ascended Master and Teacher, Kut-humi, come as *John, the Beloved,* to assist and support Jesus in his works-of-wonder?

Did he, Kut-humi, come again to assist and to support the next great wave of beautiful Light Workers who descended to the planet at the terrible time of the part of history, which became known as the *witch-hunts?*

Was Kut-humi both John, the Beloved, and Michel Nostradamus, at these vital times in Earth's recent history, during the Age of Pisces? Has this great Being-of-Light descended yet again to Earth, in order to lead these new, little ones once again? If so, will he be THE CHRIST of AQUARIUS?

This, of course, does not preclude THE CHRIST of PISCES from returning, although he may not choose to come as a child this time. Perhaps, he is here already; or, perhaps, he has never left at all!

Those who can raise their own vibratory frequency to an extremely high level will *Know* and will *See.* Those who cannot do so will either ignore or deride.

What will the *Good People of Earth* do this time around?

The answer to this question is: *it is yet to be seen.*

There is no question on how the negative ones, who control Earth, will react. They will react as they have done always – in fear. Those in fear know only one response and that is to attack.

The children of the Light and Love of God will be in their sights again, as they were in Jesus' time and as they were in the time of Nostradamus. The question that arises relates to the *Good People of Earth*, that silent majority who does not wish to become involved, because, at a personal level, their involvement could cost them dearly – perhaps even their own lives.

If the negative ones are permitted to *whip-up* mass hysteria, through their media outlets, and the majority of Earth's population *buys-into* this fear that these ones are marketing very successfully, the beautiful children of The Light and The Love of Almighty God will be targeted again. This will be simply because the beautiful ones will not allow themselves to be *pigeon-holed* and to be labelled as being of a specific religion or cause.

So, Earth stands at a pivotal point in her history. If the negative ones are given free-rein once again, few will withstand the devastation that they cause and the planet herself might be teetering on the brink of extinction.

If the *Good People of Earth* refuse to respond to the negativity and they refuse to participate in another of those *wars-to-end-all-wars*, the planet may be spared the immediate devastation that appears inevitable, at this stage.

If the *Good People of Earth* were to peel away the scales of false teachings that have been allowed to stifle Humanity's Consciousness for oh-so-long, a new dawn would arrive on Earth.

That Dawn is the Golden Age of Enlightened Consciousness.

It is on the doorstep, as are the Golden Age Babes who are beginning very tentatively and extremely hopefully to descend, via the birth experience, to Mother Earth.

Will they be received in Love and welcomed in joy and hope by a tired, tried and tested population? That is the major and burning question for the inhabitants of Earth to answer and to grapple with now.

Will the population of Earth cling desperately to outmoded ideas and ideals that belong back in Noah's Ark? Or, will they embrace the new (and age-old) philosophy of Peace on Earth and Goodwill to all?

As these *Illumined Ones*, led by THE CHRIST of the Age of Aquarius, arrive, this question will be answered – unequivocally and for all time.

The survival of the planet, known currently as *Earth*, hinges directly on the decision and on the actions of the *Good People of Earth* now.

Peace be with you. Goodwill to all!

Discourses 14

Pathways

(From the sixth book of the Series, **ERA of DISCERNMENT**)

There is a song whose words are relevant: 'If I had my life to live over, I'd walk down that same path with you.'

How many people who are incarnate on Earth now would be able to utter those same words to their current partner, husband or spouse? The answer is "not many", in all probability.

The way, in which life during any incarnation, pans out is important. What is more important, however, is the manner, in which that life was lived.

There are those on the planet who live only to satisfy their ego (self). Their only goal in life is self-gratification and the gaining of the adulation of others. Power is important to them, be that in the family setting, social setting, business setting or at a global scale. These are the ones who would be described as having a *limited consciousness*. This is not a disease that they have inherited. It is a free will choice, on their part, to play the *games-of-Earth* that they see others playing and they want a part of that action for themselves.

It was their free will choice, in earlier life-spans, to close down their higher frequency centres, or chakras, one at a time. They are free to open these centres at any time and to re-connect with their God-Source. The rub is that to do so, they must accept freely, and without reservation, their part in some of the terrible and treacherous events that have played themselves out on Earth's stage in her past history. In doing so, they have violated Cosmic Law. No law on Earth can override Cosmic Law, this being the Law-of-One.

There is one law for all, regardless of which universe or reality a person has chosen to reside. The Law-of-One is the concept of Unconditional Love. This is to treat every person in the manner that you would wish to be treated – in Love and without conditions being placed on that Love.

The ones who play power-games continuously, regardless of which particular lifetime is being scrutinised, have transgressed Cosmic Law – the Law-of-One-Love for all. These ones fear the death of their physical bodies most of all, because they never know the day or the hour when a hand will fall onto their shoulder and they will hear clearly the words: 'It is time!'

Then, their personal Akashic Records will be opened and these will be on display for all to see and to peruse. For most who *live by the sword* and who possess a very limited consciousness, this would be the moment that they have dreaded for eternity.

Within the time-frame of the Age of Aquarius, this dread will become a reality for them. Whether these ones are the monsters who have ruled the planet down through the ages, or they are their eager and willing subordinates who carry out every command effectively and efficiently, it does not matter. This is the pathway that these ones have chosen to walk along in lifetime-after-lifetime-after-lifetime.

They have closed down every chakra, within their own spirit-bodies, that operates above the Sacral chakra of Divine Power.

Others who are in embodiment on the planet watch their deeds and atrocities in horror. Afterwards, these loving Beings-of-Light move in to pick-up-the-pieces, so to speak. Most other people who are incarnate on the planet now would be operating at the level of the Heart centre. A few might be working from the Solar Plexus chakra. These are the ones who can be motivated to act in an unloving manner on occasions by the ones of the lower frequency who live by Power alone.

Some of these Power-operators may wear the garb of priest to disguise their intent and their low vibratory frequency. In this manner, they can disguise their true intent and the base nature, to which they have allowed themselves to descend.

The question that needs to be asked is this: 'if all are equal in God's Sight, how is it that one person can don the garb of priest, prince, pope or that of any other authority figure who believes that he has the right-of-kings to lead others back to God?'

Everyone knows the answer to the question. There is no need for further explanation on the matter.

It is essential for the survival of the planet and all those billions of people who reside on her, for these ones to be defeated. There is only one way that this can be done.

It is not by playing the same childish and destructive power games that they are playing. They will win every time, because they are the experts there. They have developed aggression and murderous-intent into an art form.

The only way that they can be defeated is through Love Unconditional.

So, the ones who work from the Heart chakra or higher can defeat these ones by assisting Mother Earth in her quest to *rise above* their negativity.

How can this be done? A way has been shown within the pages of this book. Everyone has the free will choice to assist, to ignore, or to find another way to assist Mother Earth in her upward spiral.

She cannot be stopped. She can be delayed. There is a saying on Earth that covers this dilemma: 'evil flourishes when good people do nothing.'

Do not give into the temptation to beat these *low* ones at their own game, I beg of you, no matter how great the temptation or how justified one feels the cause is. They cannot be beaten at that level. They invented the level.

Through meditation – alone or with others – miracles can be achieved. Those of a limited consciousness will delay Mother Earth in whatever way they can. If this means a planet-wide nuclear war, they will have no compunction in starting it. Few will be in embodiment on the planet at the end of a war such as that.

Through meditation – alone or with others – they can be defeated. A planetary healing, given in Love, can work wonders. If done secretly and silently, the element of surprise can be utilised.

A method has been shown. A way has been revealed. Through *The Rose* of Unconditional Love, all will *rise above* the turmoil of Earth, because Mother Earth will rise above the turmoil created by these individuals who work collectively to destroy her.

Our Earth Mother is *on the move*. Who is coming with her?

Adieu, sweet ones. In the peace, joy and Divine Love of Almighty God, I leave you. Enjoy your journey from here.

Discourse 15

Our Special Garden

There is a garden. It is a very special place and a sanctuary away from the cares of everyday life on Earth – that being the world of the physical.

Away from life's cares, we are free to roam and to ponder on what life is all about as we lift our spirit high. Roam with me up this slight incline. The grass is green and feels as soft as silk under foot. The sky is a brilliant blue and cloudless. The trees are green, of course, but they appear to the naked eye to have a purple hue to them, as though this is their very special auric field on display. Their aura gives a clue to the level that we are visiting this day. Only those who are capable of raising their personal vibratory frequency to a very high range can visit here. It is exclusive to those who are 'of-the-Light'.

So, welcome to this world of Love and Light!

Up ahead and a little to our left, there is a gently-flowing stream. When we draw closer, we spy a quaint, timber bridge that is quite short in length. The middle section of this bridge is quite high to allow for canoes and gondolas to glide beneath it. This could almost be a Japanese garden, if it were not for the crocodiles basking in the sunshine on the banks of the stream.

However, it is not really a stream, we realise, when we allow ourselves to look more closely. We have reached the start of the bridge now. It is spanning a moat and, on the other side, there is an island. It is only a small island, but it is dwarfed by the massive and magnificent building that takes up most of its land space. The building is a gleaming white mirage. The structure known on Earth as the Taj Mahal would fit snugly into one small section of this magnificent monument.

It is a monument to Divine and Everlasting Love.

Slowly and in awe, we cross the narrow timber bridge and step onto the carpet grass on the other side. The birdlife is in abundance. A lazy crocodile glides gracefully into the water on this day of peace and tranquillity in our special place. Squirrels scurry to and fro, paying scant notice to us. This is a place that is free from fear. To feel fear now would be to lower our vibratory frequency considerably and our garden would disappear from view instantly.

The secret hidden from view within the deepest section of this building is secure. Few can raise their vibrations to visit here.

What is the secret at its Core Centre?

It is the Holy-of-Holies

The New Jerusalem

In a short while, I will take you within its walls and we will explore its hidden core-centre together.

Before then, let us take a quick detour as we circumnavigate the gleaming white building situated on this long-forgotten island of Love.

Discourse 16

Holy of Holies –

The New Jerusalem

On a blissful morning, in a state of meditation, let us journey to our garden. We can walk on the railway sleepers on the disused railway line as we traverse the tunnel. At the end of the tunnel, we find our Spiritual Guide of Light and Love waiting for us. He or she is sitting on the chair that has been hewn from solid rock, while resting an arm on the rock table.

There is an initial greeting and a warm embrace. Feel the Unconditional Love of the Creator-of-All flowing through every fibre of your being now.

With arms linked, let us walk slowly by the massive waterfall that is covering the cliff face. Feel its gentle spray on your face and arms. Wonder at the glorious setting, into which you have entered as you study the white unicorns grazing on the bank by the edge of the stream.

Today, let us take a different path. As we trek by the waterfall while walking away from the stepping stones that lead to the swaying suspension bridge and the coffee shop, we revel in the silence. That silence is broken only by the sound of the water gushing over the massively-high cliff face and descending into the deep rock-pool beneath it.

The sound of the gushing water begins to recede as we explore a little way along our path. Lining either side of the path are fruit trees that are drooping with ripe fruit of many different varieties. We glance at the juicy pears, ripe-red apples, the oranges that resemble grapefruit in size and the grapes that drip from nearby vines.

Where is this place, we do wonder. Why have we never been here before now? The answer, of course, is that we have been here – and to places that are similar to it – many, many times. We just do not recall these occasions at a conscious level.

Through the clearing ahead of us, an expanse of water appears. It is a lake, with an island in the centre. There is a quaint timber bridge, which leads across the water to the island. This bridge is narrow and we are required to cross in single-file.

On the bank, there are crocodiles basking in the sunshine as the sun blazes down from a cloudless blue sky. There is no fear here – only Love Everlasting.

In the centre of the island is a gleaming white building. It is circular in shape and it appears to be constructed of white alabaster. There is a glass dome in the centre of its roof. It is a magnificent building by anyone's standards. The kings and queens of Earth would kill for the sheer pleasure of owning such a building and claiming it as their castle.

As we approach, we notice that there are many doorways. The first doorway has a porch-like entrance that could be the doorway to any Christian church anywhere in the world. There is a large gold cross above the door.

We move on and we pass by the next doorway, which is the entrance to a Buddhist temple/gompha, with prayer wheels and banners in evidence. We continue on our way. The next doorway resembles a Jewish synagogue, followed by the one beside it, which is a mosque.

We circle the entire building. We find that there are exactly twelve entrances and all represent exactly twelve different religions of Earth. Finding ourselves back at the first entrance again, we decide to enter this one and to explore a little inside its interior.

Before we do so, we sit on the grass momentarily. The crocodiles pay scant attention to us as the birds flit from tree to tree. An inquisitive monkey approaches slowly before retreating to a nearby tree, having found something more interesting to hold its attention.

The peace and tranquillity of the setting is soul-soothing. After a time, we rise – as one – and we walk slowly beneath the gold cross of the Christian entrance of the building.

Crossing beneath the cross at the threshold, we walk inside and discover that it could be any Christian church anywhere in the world. We sit down on the front timber pew and side-by-side we study the white marble altar before us. There is a picture hanging on the wall near to us. The image is depicting the last supper of The Christ, with his apostles in attendance.

A slight breeze wafts through the open door behind us. Its gentle flow lifts the curtain slightly and it brushes against the altar. In this brief moment, we spy a doorway behind the curtain.

Leaving our Guide seated on the front pew, we move forward, full of curiosity. We lift the curtain and touch the door handle lightly. This slight touch is sufficient to release the catch and the door swings open silently.

Without glancing back to our Guide, we enter the Holy-of-Holies!

In awe, we move forward. The feelings that we experience here are so soul-soothing that we feel The Pulsing begin to activate the Heart chakra within the centre of our being. Momentarily transfixed, we study our surroundings and we are surprised to notice that we are not alone. There are eleven other doorways. All are entrances from all of the other religious places of worship. We are stunned by this realisation. Then, we notice that there are twelve angels standing by the twelve doors and we understand how it was that our door opened so easily at our gentle touch. All the doors are closed, with the exception of the one, through which we have entered this holy place.

The entire room is circular. On the white marble floor, in the centre, is a golden star, set in a circle of gold. Mesmerised as much by the grandeur as by the colossal size of the room where we stand, we move towards the star in a trance-like state. Overhead, sunlight streams in through the clear glass dome.

The sun's rays dance upon the golden star and its surrounding circle of Light.

With our head tilted back slightly, we stare up through the roof and we study the azure blue of the cloudless sky. What a perfect world, we marvel.

There is a light touch upon our hands. Our Guide is standing directly behind us. We feel our arms being raised in the air. As the most intoxicating feelings of Love infuse us, soft thoughts enter our minds. These are thought-projections from our Guide.

"Draw up the Divine Love of God from the well deep within."

"Draw down the Divine Light of God from our Alpha Point above."

"Ignite the Violet Flame of Love at our Diamond-Centre within."

"Direct the beam of Divine Love and Light – the Christ Light – to pour forth into the Heart Centre of Mother Earth."

Following these gentle instructions while closing our eyes, we feel as though the skirt of a hovercraft is inflating beneath our feet. Our arms are stretched towards the heavenly sky above us and, together, we resemble the letter 'Y' of the English language of Earth.

In this blissful state-of-Being, we remain as The Pulsing continues unabated. The Quickening raises our vibratory frequency as we drift higher inside the dome. Opening our eyes, we realise that we are linked still – as the One Being – but, we are above the glass of the dome.

We float effortlessly for a little while – as a cloud in the sky would do – before gliding gracefully and slowly to the ground where we had been resting previously, before entering the building. The experience was almost surreal, yet we knew – deep within our Being – that we had experienced this glorious union with our Guide many times before this moment.

A fleeting thought enters our mind as we study our Guide while in a trance-like state still.

"Are you my Guide or my Twin Flame?"

"I AM both. We are the One Being. We have been always. We will be always. There is no moment when we are separate. You can be the Twin Flame of no other. I can be the Twin Flame of no other. We were breathed into Life by our Creator-God as the One Being in one moment. All others are soul-mates or, as called sometimes, twin-souls. These are ones from the same soul-family who incarnate together over and over and over again, for one specific purpose. That is to bring the Love and to expand and extend that Love to all who reside on a darkened planet."

"And, this magnificent building on this peaceful island?" we ask, through our thought-projections.

"It is available and open to all at any time, any day, any night. Its doors are never closed. The entrance, through which one chooses to come, is a free will choice."

"It represents many religions," we mention the obvious.

"Beliefs are many. The New Jerusalem is available to all. The New Jerusalem has arrived on Earth. All that is required by ones who wish to avail themselves of the peace, tranquillity and Love that permeates its space is to raise one's vibratory frequency to the point where one can see and feel its glory; where one can feel the Divine Love of God within its walls while floating in Divine Light. Once discovered, enter through the doorway of your choice. Feel Divine Love infuse you completely. Allow Divine Light to lift you to even greater heights as you float in Its Rays. Ignite the Violet Flame that lies dormant within everyone in embodiment on Earth now. Visit the sanctuary of Love and re-connect, for a short while, with your one-and-only Twin Flame. In Divine Light, you will find your way here. Through Divine Wisdom and Divine Will, you will *Know* the timing of your visit to coincide with the arrival of your precious other-half. Lost in Divine Love, you will re-connect as Divine Order brings Balance between the two, making two halves whole again. Divine Power and Divine Life will be subservient, belonging solely to the lower bodies. Only on Earth are these lower frequencies used – and more often than not, abused – as the ego seeks to make the higher bodies subservient to it. Its success in this ongoing endeavour is borne out by the state that Mother Earth endures today. End her suffering. Slowly, silently and imperceptibly, lower The New Jerusalem to Earth. The Mother – this being Earth – cannot do so alone. Her vibratory frequency is at a very low ebb now, due to the dense negativity of the ones who exploit her relentlessly. It falls to the children-of-Light to bring the frequency of this special place to Earth now. Then, as a bride on her wedding day, Mother Earth can re-connect with Father Sky, in a grand reunion. Those of a lower vibration will not be able to remain within this rarefied atmosphere, brought on by the sublime combination of *Divine Love, Divine Light and The Violet Flame.*"

Buoyed by the ecstatic experience and enlightened by the explanation of our Guide and Twin Flame, we rise. In silence, we cross the timber bridge as one or two crocodiles glide slowly and effortlessly into the water. We continue on our way and return to the waterfall. We walk to the tunnel entrance where we embrace our Twin Flame in a fond farewell. We enter the darkened tunnel alone and we return slowly and somewhat reluctantly to the position where we left our physical bodies resting while being bathed in the protective Light of our personal pyramid-of-Light. It is being guarded by the Guardians-of-Light whom we called to stand beside and above our empty shell when we left our physical body to explore in the higher realm – vibrationally-speaking, of course.

Thanking our special Spiritual Guides, as well as the Guardians-of-Light, we re-enter our resting physical form. Slowly, one-by-one, we close our chakras to pinpoints of Light while sealing our auric field in a bubble, pyramid or shield of Light before going on with our day.

The New Jerusalem awaits. Come one and all. Come in Love. There is no other way to reach this heavenly haven – our Jerusalem-on-High!

In God's Love,

Adieu.

Discourse 17

The Illumined Ones

(From the sixth book of the Series, **ERA of DISCERNMENT**)

The gentleness of the Golden Age babes will be the first notable sign of their identity.

They will be without guile, so it will be easy for others to hoodwink them on occasions, because they will assume that all others are without guile, also. When they come to realise, at a conscious level, that other people who are around them, are plotting and planning future events for the satisfaction of the ego-self, these little ones will not respond similarly. They *Know*, at the deepest level, that they are here for one reason only. That is to give *service* to the First Cause.

Through their unending service, they will provide Love and support to others, asking for nothing in return. They are attuned solely to Divine Will, just as Jesus was during his life, and they will offer a similar service, as he did. How they will be received is yet to be seen.

If they receive the same treatment as he did, at the hands of ones who operate solely from Divine Power and ego, they will withdraw back to Spirit – one-by-one – and Humanity collectively will be left to its own devices. They will not remain in embodiment to suffer a similar fate to what was metered out to them in the time of Nostradamus.

These little ones will choose parents who are kind and loving. More importantly, they will choose parents whose minds are open to new ideas and concepts, which in truth, are age-old concepts that have been abandoned by a world that is subservient to the technological monsters that it has developed. Reliance on these great technological dinosaurs of twentieth-century ingenuity will be the downfall of many in a time to come.

When the technological and the scientific advances of a civilisation have reached a point where such advances have outstripped the philosophical and spiritual aspects of life, there is one event only that can occur. That particular civilisation is on 'borrowed-time'.

When information is released gradually and silently, in the form of ideas coming from Divine Light (Illumination), it is wise to acknowledge the Original Source. Unfortunately, this happens rarely as the ones making the discoveries are usually coming from the perspective of the ego, so they accept all kudos as the rightful acknowledgement of their great achievements in the scientific world. Seldom is it recognised that perhaps a Higher Source released the information to an over-active, scientific mind, because it was considered – in the Higher Realms – that Humanity was ready to receive and to benefit from this next step in its evolution.

Giving accolades to the First Cause, Who is God Everlasting, is not high on the priorities of those whose scientific minds cannot conceive of a Force and a Source more powerful and possessing more Wisdom than that of the receiver of the information.

At a time when these breakthroughs are considered necessary, for the benefit of those who are incarnate on Earth, it is tragic to watch the by-products of these so-called *new* inventions being utilised to aid the negative cause on the planet.

There have been many such incidents, during the period of the twenty and twenty-first centuries. The information that was released was done so in the hope that its uses would be positive, bringing about loving and caring outcomes for the population as a whole.

During the Age of Pisces, these new little ones who are fresh to life on Planet Earth now, came at least twice before and they were slaughtered on both occasions. This was done in the most cruel and public way possible at the time. This was a warning to these Great Beings of Light that they would meet the same fate, if they should be so bold as to come a third time, at the beginning of Aquarius, in order to rescue a sleepy population who has given its power away to a negative force that controls every aspect of life on Earth.

This time, the negative ones will be refused permission to return to Earth in another physical embodiment, once their current physical body has worn out with age, or has been destroyed by others of their ilk. Their co-conspirators who replace them usually and who are waiting *in the wings* to descend again, through the birth experience, will be denied this opportunity for at least one thousand years of Earth-time.

Perhaps, the time has arrived for all of their Akashic Records to be opened to full scrutiny. The *Good People of Earth* have nothing to fear from the opening of their Akashic Records. This is due to the fact that they operate on a 'pay-as-you-go' system where karmic consequences are concerned. The ones to whom I refer as 'the negative force' are the ones who have refused point-blank to repay karmic debt for thousands upon thousands of years. It would be impossible for them to do so now, on a third dimensional planet – as Earth is now – and remain sane at the same time. Their debts are massive and these are beyond their ability to repay in the time available.

Earth is raising herself, through a supreme effort on her part, to a fourth dimensional entity once again. The ones who are attempting to keep her at their level, for obvious reasons, will be required to leave the premises, in a short space of time, via the death process. Perhaps then, the great day of reckoning that they have been dreading for thousands-upon-thousands of Earth years, will have arrived for them. They will do everything in their power to delay such an event occurring. If it means destroying the planet – or part thereof – they will do so. It is their own survival that is at stake here – and that is not only in a physical sense!

The Good People of Earth have much to look forward to and much to be proud of with regard to their achievements over the millennia. They have held the fort, so to speak, when all was descending into chaos around them. They have done so, in the Love of God, although most would not admit this fact publicly. They have been following their Intuitive Self, when the ego-self was demanding that they take a different course, in the interests of self-preservation. Every one of them needs to stand up and take a bow. They have held out against impossible odds in the face of great adversity, as the world was brought to-the-brink on many occasions as the great negative masters sought to take over the world and to inflict their philosophy or religion on a sleepy population. It is *sleepy* only from the perspective of Awakening to True Reality, brought on by many false teachings over time. These false teachings have been permitted to become entrenched. Nothing but the greatest of upheavals will bring this sorry chapter of Earth's history to a close.

So, this is a review of past and current situations on Earth, from the perspective of those who gaze from the heights of Spirit (at a higher frequency) and who view, with horror, the events that have happened and those that are occurring still.

On a positive note, our beautiful ones are beginning to descend. They will be insightful, clear-thinking individuals who are attuned solely to Divine Will and Divine Light while being infused with Divine Love. They can operate in Love only and they will *turn the other cheek* always.

They will position themselves on all of the major energy points of the world. They will choose parents whose minds and hearts are open to Unconditional Love. They will be like a breath of fresh air that floods into a room when a window is opened suddenly. They will be less than one hundred and fifty thousand in number. They will draw to themselves other children-of-Light who are incarnate on the planet and who are awaiting their arrival with breathless anticipation – at a spirit-level, that is. At a conscious level, our children-of-Light, in most cases, are as unaware as the rest of Earth's population that our beautiful Illumined Ones are on the move.

As like-attracts-like, our Illumined Ones will be as a lighthouse on a darkened ocean. They will draw to themselves all those who are lost and struggling on life's dark ocean. Their beacons-of-Light will flash. The children-of-Light will respond.

This is how the world will change, possibly in the space of one generation. The negative ones will have lost their battle and returned to their world of darkness, there to face their deepest and darkest fear. They were responsible for every atrocity that has occurred. They were responsible for the removal of the passages relating to reincarnation from The Bible and this act alone has cost Earth's population dearly. It gave great power to the negative ones as they controlled the minds of the population. It brought great sadness to the soul-spirit of every child-of-Light who knew, at the deepest level within, that there was another way and another truth.

A point-of-no-return has been reached. Follow the directives of the negative ones who control this planet, for their own selfish ends, and all is lost. Follow the soft, gentle, kind and loving Voice of the Spirit-Within and *Come Home* to us in triumph at the conclusion of this life-experience on Planet Earth.

These are the only two options available now to the Good People of Earth. The arguments of the negative ones will be powerful and persuasive, as they were at the time of the so-called *witch-hunts*. If the majority of the population *buys into* their messages of fear and ignorance, all is lost.

Listen-Within and follow the Light-Workers who will position themselves, as great Beacons-of-Light, on one hundred and forty-four thousand major energy centres, and the planet will rise up to God as a beautiful bride on her wedding day, bathed in the Love and Light of a grateful and astounded population.

The sight will be awesome and awe-inspiring. The children-of-Light will *Come Home to God*, along with her, and they will come en-masse. Only those who are steeped in fear and negativity will be left floundering in her wake.

Truly, it will be a magnificent sight and one that will cause all of the creations in all of God's great universes to stand still and to watch in amazement and wonder.

The *Transition Time* is upon Earth now. This period of great upheaval is necessary and unavoidable, just as the darkness before the breaking of the dawn of a new day is unavoidable.

After the Transition, Divine Light and Divine Love will flood Earth and The Mother will glow with a brilliance that is blinding to the eyes of those who behold her.

Earth is on the move. She is rising fast. She cannot be delayed or stopped now. As Aquarius dawns so, too, does her moment of supreme and sublime glory dawn.

Praise be to Almighty God!

The question that every individual, who is incarnate on Earth now, needs to ask of oneself is: "Am I rising with her – my beautiful Mother?"

Peace be with you. Goodwill to All!

This is the Final Discourse for the Series.

God Speed, Gentle Starseeds

God speed, gentle starseeds,
so trusting, so true;
God speed, gentle starseeds,
in all that you do.

Your paths are so narrow,
so tiresome, so dark;
you long for security
as your road you embark.

Come, gentle starseeds,
take My Hand as you go
to tomorrow's new landscape;
wherever life does flow.

Come, gentle starseeds,
leave all in the past.
Your thoughts turn to Home
as you open your hearts.

Allow God's Love to infuse,
to inspire and transform.
Come, gentle starseeds,
as God's Love you do draw.

You'll find a good reason
to follow your dreams.
Come, gentle starseeds,
follow where I do lead.

God Speed, Gentle Starseeds

My Heart's overflowing
with Love for you all.
God speed, gentle starseeds,
hold My Hand lest you fall.

God speed, gentle starseeds,
over land, over sea,
in city or country,
lands war-torn or free.

God speed, gentle starseeds,
come softly to Me.
In sweet, sweet surrender,
God speed thee to Me.

Stella McMillan
26 December, 2001

Author's Note

By Way of Explanation

As the author, I have battled over the release of the Discourses for many, many months. Several were released in the earlier books of the *Stella McMillan* Series. However, these have been repeated here and in sequence.

Upon reflection, the books of the first Trilogy, along with the first book of the second Trilogy, may appeal to readers of romantic fiction. The last two books of the second trilogy may interest those who are searching for a deeper meaning to current life situations.

These Discourses present another perspective again. I decided to withhold many of them from the earlier books, as the words are direct and to the point. There is nothing that is new within the pages of these Discourses. It is simply that the content is presented in a different way and it may send some people into fear. I hope that this is not the case.

As for Paula, by the conclusion of the sixth book, she was coming to an understanding that would have been beyond her comprehension just a few years earlier. Here, in the tale of this couple's forever-long love affair, we have but one example of the Cosmic Law of Cause-and-Effect in action. If one is in embodiment on the planet now, there is a legitimate reason for being here. Whether or not we acknowledge the fact to ourselves at a conscious level, whilst in physical form, is irrelevant. The truth is that we are all playing out our own personal dramas as we travel slowly along our own unique road to spiritual enlightenment. The learning of the one and only lesson there is – that being the lesson of Unconditional Love – is extremely important. There is no other reason for being here, except for the repayment of previous karmic debts.

According to the Discourses, for many, this will be insignificant and, perhaps, can be re-negotiated while being carried out on another level in-between incarnations on Earth. This is contrary to popular belief, of course, because it is assumed that we are all so-called sinners who need to repent and to return to the fold – although to which *fold* is a matter of conjecture.

Karmic Debt

In all probability, every belief-system since time began on this planet was regarded by its followers as the one-and-only *True Religion*. This view would have been promoted widely, especially by its leaders who may have had a vested interest in the total acceptance of this so-called *universal truth* within the ranks of its believers.

In some religions, along with this belief eventually would have come the one regarding the *one-life-only* concept, by which the followers of the *One True Religion* – in order to become *perfect* – must abide. The doctrines and dogma, which were being promoted by the priests/clergy of the day while being propped up by the rulers of their society in many cases (because it was in their interests to do so), would have been presented powerfully as the only way back to God.

When these two concepts of the *One True Religion* and the *one-life-only* belief are combined, they make an almost overwhelming case for accepting the doctrines as outlined by the leaders of that particular religion while placing great power in their hands. If the overall leader, or perhaps the king, were to be promoted as being infallible, it would be even more effective. So, has anything changed really?

To this day, many people continue to bury-their-heads and to pretend that this is the only lifetime that we have; therefore, we must live it to the fullest degree possible and to accumulate as much wealth as is possible, as well as acquiring as many possessions and perhaps just as many titles, honours and degrees as time will allow.

When the current physical body dies, all our wealth and possessions are passed on to others while our certificates and degrees gather dust somewhere until they are destroyed eventually by a later generation. Consequently, this becomes nothing more than an endless, futile cycle or treadmill – as these Discourses mention.

By accepting, at a conscious level, that we have one life only, we can avoid coming to terms with the true reason for this incarnation in physical form. If we all continue to play these endless, illusionary games, nothing much can be achieved personally, in a spiritual sense. In Reality, our spiritual life is the all-important one. Everything else is transitory.

Of course, some of us may have become somewhat stuck along the way on our spiritual journey. This event can occur for a number of reasons, but often it is as a result of our failure to accept the karmic consequences of certain unfortunate past incidents or actions on our part. This means that, between incarnations, we are compelled to return to a lower level on the Astral plane than we would have done otherwise. In denying those debts, we are denying ourselves the chance to reclaim our original birthright.

As the Discourses stress, it is our birthright to reside at the highest level possible between incarnations. The existence of an accrued and overdue karmic debt, along with our inability to understand the spiritual path that we are walking presently, means we restrict ourselves spiritually. To advance spiritually, we need to understand, also, the important part that our energy centres (points/chakras) play in this scenario. In order to reclaim our birthright, we need to raise our own vibratory-frequency to the highest degree possible. Our energy centres are the key to the manner, in which we commence this process. These need to be healed. We possess many energy centres within our bodies, but there are seven major ones. These are well-documented in other literature, so there is no need to elaborate further here.

When one of these major centres is closed, partially blocked or spinning in reverse, we are likely to develop an illness or an ailment within the corresponding region of the physical body eventually. If most of our higher chakras (from the Heart centre upwards) are blocked or closed partially, we are operating at a much lower frequency than we would do, under normal circumstances. These blockages have a direct bearing on our vibratory-frequency, thereby lowering the vibratory level of our auric field. This could explain the need to *keep our lamps burning brightly*.

The colours and the sounds emanating from our own aura will depict the level, to which we are restricted on our return to the Astral plane. As with a fingerprint, every aura is different and distinct. Every person has an aura that gives off a different colour, or a slightly different hue – as well as emitting a different soundwave – from everyone else. However, the Astral plane is made up of many levels. As water finds its own level, so too, do we at the conclusion of every lifetime.

To assist in the releasing, clearing and healing of the blockages that exist, Paula was shown *The Lighthouse* by her Guide, Gerard. The reason that this place was revealed to her was so that she could visit there in her meditation sessions and relax within a particular colour while on the level that would correspond with the chakra/centre/point that she felt needed healing at the time. It was her choice from there whether or not she wished to avail herself of this chance to release, clear, cleanse and heal any particular centre in her own body, so as to raise her own vibrations to a higher frequency. In so doing, the colours of her aura would be heightened greatly.

Let us use Paula as an example as we attempt to take an overview of these matters, in order to gain a little more understanding of these spiritual issues. These have been clouded in secrecy for thousands of years and their existence was unknown to most ordinary folk who, it was considered by the *Initiated*, to be ignorant and unintelligent, in many cases.

In these more enlightened times when many people are opening up to the new energies that are flooding the planet, some are beginning to question. Much of the literature available is confusing and inconsistent. In the western world, there are but a few religions that embrace the reincarnation theory, so where does the genuine seeker turn? It is to Inner Guidance, emanating from within one's own being. By following one's guidance system, direction will be given. The appropriate book, course or philosophy will appear in due course. All that is needed is to begin the quest in faith, with an open heart and mind during the exploration period.

Returning to Paula's story, we can see how she progressed from one lifetime to the next. After the Scottish life had concluded, *Fiona* returned to the physical realm once again. This time, it was as Louisa and in the country known as Australia. *Louisa* returned, in physical form once more, but in a different country yet again. This time, she came as a citizen of America and she was given the name of *Paula*.

Within the pages of these fictitious novels, we have followed the stories of the various lifetimes when she possessed other names/identities. At the end of every lifetime, she returned to her other life and those identities were discarded, along with the physical form, which she had utilised for the duration of that sojourn. All the names, titles, honours, diplomas and wealth, which she won or held during every incarnation, ceased to exist. These disappeared, along with the former and temporary identity, by which she was acknowledged, once the recently-discarded physical body was required no longer by her. So, who is she really? She must have an ongoing identity – a Higher Self/I AM Presence – by which she is known, and has been known, since before time began.

Of course, she does. When she awakens from the dream-sequence, (or, perhaps, the nightmare), which is life-on-Earth for her in any incarnation, she will assume her true identity. Paula will return to her home that is waiting there for her, as we all do. She will resume her real identity and, more importantly, her forever-long, never-ending spirit-life until she decides to seek another adventure on the plane of Earth.

In True Reality, who is the one that we have come to know as Fiona/Louisa/Paula?

She is, of course, the beautiful Selene!

Image of 'The Child'

Several years ago, when I discovered the image of the child in the forefront of the painting of *The Last Supper* by Leonardo da Vinci, my initial reactions were similar to those that I described previously as occurring with Paula in the book, **ERA of DISCERNMENT.** I was astonished, to say the least. *Spellbound* would be closer to the mark, I would suggest. Having been educated at a Catholic college and having received strict instruction in the Catholic faith, I was no stranger to this painting. In fact, at the time of the discovery of the boy-child kneeling on the table, I could place my hands instantly on two similar books on my bookshelf. Having verified the image in those other books and subsequently with a friend, I placed it aside and continued on with the re-writes of my Series. Perhaps, the implications of this revelation were too much for my conscious mind to process at the time.

This realisation had come about when I was reading a fictitious novel that I had stumbled across in a bookstore. It was a tale of intrigue set in the church and monastery where Leonardo was creating his masterpiece and it involved an Officer of The Inquisition who had been sent from Rome to investigate. The author was Javier Sierra. The original story was written in Spanish and translated into English by Alberto Manguel. The title was: *The Secret Supper A Novel.* In fact, it was the cover that drew my attention to the book. The front and back covers depicted *The Last Supper.* Both covers opened out fully and inside, there was another copy of the painting. The cover photographs were attributed to Eva Pastor.

I included my astounding discovery in the sixth book of this Series for the benefit of those who have not witnessed the startling image for themselves. I cannot convince myself of the fact that I could be the first to discover the image. It is not possible. I am certain that this has been a closely guarded secret within certain quarters for a long, long time. Did Leonardo da Vinci know a deep secret, about which the rest of us have been denied knowledge for many, many centuries? Possibly, this is so.

Two Trilogies

The question that I have been asked often is in regard to the titles of these separate novels that I have been writing over the past four decades. I will attempt an explanation here.

The **ERROR of UNDERSTANDING**, as well as the **ERROR PERPETUATED**, relates to the belief in the concept of one-life-only in order to become the perfect person while walking around in physical form. From the viewpoint of ones who lived during the Age of Pisces, this was accepted as *truth* by many. Any person who dared to query such a well-known belief was labelled as either deranged or a heretic who was out to tear asunder the established order. The fact that reincarnation was a part of the Bible originally was not accepted. The possibility that the Bible could have been altered in any way would have been regarded as a scandalous suggestion. Whispered words would have been the only means to promote this theory.

With Leonardo da Vinci who was working as an artist at the time of the Inquisition, he would have been required to create his paintings in such a way that these works of art would stand the test of time. The suggestion that the person who was seated beside Jesus in *The Last Supper* was a female and that she could have been depicting Mary of Magdala – the Magdalene – would have seen him meet an excruciating and horrendous death at the hands of the cruellest of men, regardless of the garb that they were wearing in everyday life. That he painted a small child, and probably a boy-child, kneeling on the table in that scene – and, what's more, he lived beyond its subsequent public exhibition – is testament to his courage and his brilliance, as well as giving a clue to his beliefs at the time.

It was a time of *limited consciousness* back then. This situation has changed little, it would seem. In many quarters, this limited consciousness applies still. By publications and novels such as these, another perspective is shown. The concept of reincarnation will be re-established firmly in this Age of Aquarius. The new, little ones who are coming to Earth in great numbers, through the birth process now, will not be able to accept the one-life-only theory. As stated in the Discourses, their vibratory frequency is too high for them to accept such a limited viewpoint. In their hearts, they will know that, in reality, it is otherwise. This will be in the time-frame that I call the **ERA of UNDERSTANDING**.

With a more enlightened population inhabiting the planet, an **AWAKENING TO AWARENESS** is imminent. It is vital then that when these new little babies who are known, also, as the *Golden Age Babes* – or, sometimes even described as *The Illumined Ones* – arrive in their new physical bodies that they come to parents who are *open* and *aware*.

If they were to be born to ones who were of the limited consciousness of a bygone era, they would begin to suffocate very quickly, as the Discourses suggest. Perhaps then, some may choose to return to the Astral plane of Spirit very soon after their arrival, due to severe breathing difficulties or suffocation that may not have been caused by an obvious physical condition.

With regard to this Series of books, it may be that an **ERROR PROFOUND** is discovered when another perspective is presented and this is found to be more plausible to ones who are of an *expanded*, or possibly even an *enlightened*, consciousness. Presently, in this **ERA of DISCERNMENT**, many will realise the truth of the matter. Whether they are prepared to accept and/or to act on this newly-discovered concept – new to them, that is, while being older than time itself – is to be seen.

After all, it took a traumatic event, accompanied by an out-of-body experience, to bring Paula to an awakened awareness. Her children will be the beneficiaries of her enlightened consciousness from this point onwards. She appears to be coaxing a sceptical Lachlan along with her on her spiritual journey towards understanding and enlightenment in a way that Louisa could never have hoped to achieve with the rational, logical and worldly Charles Lyndhurst of their nineteenth century lifetime.

It all comes down to one's perspective, I suppose. In this new age, many of us might find ourselves in situations where we may need to take one giant leap of faith. This hair-raising and breath-taking leap could take us from where we stand now, with our firmly-held religious beliefs and our conscious minds, which have been clouded and conditioned by outmoded concepts that became entrenched during the fast-departing Piscean Age, to the place where we land – hopefully on both feet – in this present Age of Aquarius.

For those who are inquisitive of nature, as well as being open, courageous and possessing minds that probe relentlessly, the Discourses presented here, in this book, may bring further enlightenment, although I suspect that some will find them disconcerting, to say the least.

Reincarnation

Considering the subject of reincarnation for a moment, this is a basic tenet of the Buddhist faith, which was founded around the teachings of the very wise sage and holy man, Gautama Siddhartha, who lived around 500 BC.

Within the Christian teachings, the theory of reincarnation is regarded with suspicion and ridicule. This was not always the case. Almost all traces of reincarnation were removed deliberately and systematically by the Emperor Justinian of Constantinople (now Istanbul), along with the elders of the Church, at the second church council of Nicaea in 553AD – although many dispute vehemently the fact that this act occurred. In the Bible today, there are a few passages that escaped this careful cropping and these have been documented in other publications. Subsequently, other groups broke away from Rome and formed other branches of Christianity; but, for the most part, these new churches kept to the Roman text – *after* the removal of the passages pertaining to reincarnation.

There are two questions that need to be asked by those who are seeking answers of a spiritual nature.

The first one relates to the witch-hunts that occurred mid-way through the Age of Pisces. Would the ones who were committed to the teachings of Christianity, have perpetrated those barbaric, sadistic and cruel acts of torture and death on innocent people if they had known that reincarnation was a fact of life and that a karmic debt was attached to their dreadful and dastardly deeds at that time?

Secondly, let us consider the ones who were the self-appointed religious leaders and who were responsible for spurring on the demented mobs that caused this widespread carnage. If those religious leaders had been in possession of the knowledge, regarding the previous removal of passages from the Bible, would these leaders have baulked at altering any other part of the Bible, if it suited their cause at the time? They appeared to have no compunction in killing their innocent victims, in a terrible and horrendous manner, simply because someone had labelled those people as witches.

To this day, committed Christians are awaiting the return of the one known as Jesus, The Christ, in physical form. Those of the Jewish religion are awaiting the arrival of the promised Messiah. Buddhists are awaiting the return of The Buddha (Gautama Siddhartha) whom they believe, at a higher level, is known as The Lord Maitreya.

For ones whose minds are open and who are prepared to face the possibility that reincarnation is a definite fact of life, they might wish to take a few moments to contemplate the following: (a) that the removal of all traces of – as well as a belief in the theory of – reincarnation from the Bible was a deliberate act carried out for the purpose of keeping control of the illiterate masses. After all, the only ones who were allowed to possess a copy of the Bible, in those early days, were the priests. All others were forbidden from holding or owning one; and

(b) that, if reincarnation is a fact-of-life, all those from other faiths may be awaiting the arrival/birth/return of the same individual. This could be a case of the divide-and-rule principle in action. There is another sobering thought.

The subject of censorship of religious documents brings to the fore another question, which came to light in recent times in the book, THE HOLY BLOOD AND THE HOLY GRAIL, by the authors: Michael Baigent, Richard Leigh and Henry Lincoln. In the above-mentioned publication, these authors posed many pertinent questions, which sent my mind reeling and racing at once. As with many other readers, I began to ask myself if it was possible that the humble, gentle, loving and wise Jewish man, J'shua bar Joseph, who was known as the prophet, Jesus, and who became The Christ of the Piscean Age, had married Mary of Magdala, at the marriage feast at Cana.

Mary, the Magdalene, has been labelled as a fallen woman. According to the American author and theologian, Bart D. Ehrman, in his book, *'Peter, Paul and Mary Magdalene* THE FOLLOWERS OF JESUS IN HISTORY AND LEGEND', it was Pope Gregory The Great who gathered together all of the stories relating to a woman called Mary in the Bible. Then, he delivered a sermon, in which he attributed all the negative aspects and actions of this composite woman to Mary Magdalene. Presumably then, confirmation of the revelation regarding her marriage to Jesus, if it were proven to be true, would cause something of a furore, I expect, as well as bringing into question the need for priests of the Roman Catholic Church to be celibate in the first place. What a stir that would cause!

As I studied in detail a copy of Leonardo da Vinci's painting of *The Last Supper*, which was scrutinised carefully by the authors of the book, THE HOLY BLOOD AND THE HOLY GRAIL, a different picture emerged. There was the knot that was displayed there and this was tied in the corner of the cloth covering the table. Supposedly, this knot was a symbol, which Leonardo used whenever Mary Magdalene was depicted. The person seated beside Jesus, in the painting, was supposed to be the apostle, John the Beloved, although in recent times this has been alleged to be Mary Magdalene.

So, my mind commenced its cartwheels once again as I began to wonder where John would be, in the painting of *The Last Supper*, if the person who was seated beside Jesus was indeed Mary of Magdala. Jesus had twelve apostles and there were only thirteen people present at the supper. I asked myself who was missing from the picture then. Certainly, it would not be John, because he was very special to Jesus. Then, I observed the disembodied hand, which was holding a dagger.

I pondered on this symbol while finally coming to the conclusion that perhaps this was meant to represent the missing Judas Iscariot. Therefore, the one who was sitting slightly in front of Mary could be John the Beloved, because the one leaning behind him, and towards Mary, was stated to be the apostle, Peter. This persistent thought brought with it another possible conclusion. This was: if Judas had left the gathering already, to carry out his terrible act of the betrayal of Jesus, this painting of *The Last Supper* could be depicting the aftermath of the supper; or, it was the supper in its closing stages.

While I was lost in these astounding deliberations, I was *drifting* once again, I suppose. Then, I gasped aloud in astonishment – as I am certain that many, many thousands of people before me, over the past five or six centuries, have done when they witnessed what my eyes were revealing to me. I gasped in appreciation of not only the brilliance of Leonardo da Vinci, as the artist who had created this superb masterpiece, but also at the audacity of the man!

Under the noses of the Officers of the Inquisition, he had made a definite statement. It was a shocking, preposterous revelation. Such a statement and revelation could have seen him arrested and brought before the stern and officious Officers of Pope Alexander VI, charged with heresy and burnt at the stake. However, he was too clever for all of them.

Supposedly, one of the main criticisms levelled at Leonardo by Church officials of the time was that there was no chalice, or Holy

Grail, to represent the vessel holding the Holy Blood of Christ visible on the table and that the Eucharist, which is a central part of the holy mass, was not in view either. However, I beg to differ. Once my concentrated gaze was focussed fully on the apostle, who was seated directly in front of Peter, I was astounded to witness the *Holy Grail* who was there on the table in the painting, *The Last Supper*. The *vessel*, draped in blue garments, was visible clearly indeed.

There, kneeling on the table, directly in front of the one who I had concluded was the apostle, John, (although named always as Judas) was *a child!*

The child was very young and he was dressed in garments that were blue in colour; so, presumably, this was meant to depict a *boy-child*. Also, close by, there appeared to be a disembodied hand, which was holding a dagger. Above this hand, a face was visible although it was almost lost in the garments of one of the apostles. It was all very intriguing. However, the one who has been labelled always as being Judas was holding a money bag supposedly containing his ill-gotten gains. Suddenly, before my astounded eyes, this money bag became the forearm of the young boy.

Now, whenever I look at this colour photograph of the painting, *The Last Supper*, all that I can see is this child. My eyes gravitate towards him immediately. However, for many decades, I had looked at this same image and, always, I had seen Jesus, with six men on his right and six men on his left – *and nothing else.*

It is all in one's perspective, I suppose, as Lachlan Jefferson stated often. I cannot view this particular copy of the painting without witnessing Mary seated at the right side of Jesus while the young boy is kneeling on the table, slightly in front of this seated couple. Yet, this is an astounding image that I had never noticed before I purchased this particular book, despite all of the years that I was involved with Christianity.

Since then, I have studied other copies of the painting, *The Last Supper*, by Leonardo da Vinci. Always, I see Mary Magdalene and the boy-child in every one of them. I suppose we see only that which we want to see, most of the time. Sometimes, the obvious is staring us in the face and we are blind to it. All of this information, I revealed previously in my earlier books of this Series.

The Catholic faith, as practised by ones with love and peace in their hearts, is a beautiful religion. The Jewish people who practise the Jewish faith, along with all those ones who are devoted to Buddhism and to many of the other religions of the world, are genuine and loving souls who are fellow-companions on life's spiritual journey. Perhaps, as with our Paula who had been the very Catholic Louisa in a previous life, we have all been followers of these various religions in different and past incarnations while, this time around, we continue to explore other philosophies, concepts and religions.

Unfortunately, some members of the hierarchy of one of those establishments cannot be seen in this light any longer by ones with minds that are open and questioning. This top-heavy establishment has become a giant, lurching ship, which has been holed below the water-line, due to its persistent cover-up of dreadful and despicable crimes that have come out into the open of late.

The sincere, innocent and loving members of its crew, along with the dedicated followers and their devoted family members are crying out for assistance as the waters of the sea soak its decking. Many of its numerous first officers appear to be oblivious to the terrible plight of those genuine, caring ones who are below-deck while, on the upper deck, they continue to believe that it is *business-as-usual* – as it has been for hundreds of years of Earth-time. This massive, ancient Titanic is sinking slowly beneath the waves. Presently, *The See* seems to be on the verge of being swallowed up in a sea of complete indifference and utter contempt. Could it be that it has become simply a relic of the old, receding Piscean Age?

Those ones who are *of-the-Light* and who have chosen to follow in the footsteps of the soft, gentle, kind and loving Jesus – whether they choose to follow the Catholic faith, or another branch of the Christian religion – are intelligent, caring, loving souls who are able to *discern* for themselves the truth of the matter. In times past, this very act of discernment could have seen them burnt at the stake. In many cases, it did.

By the labelling of many of the children-of-Light as witches, this covered a multitude of sins, I suspect. Those who are of an expanded consciousness and who possess minds that probe deeply in search of truth have lost faith in organised religions, for the most part.

With the Age of Aquarius, the tenets of the old titanic have become obsolete. Its parishioners are no longer the illiterate masses. They are thinking, caring, discerning and loving individuals, some of whom are – or, soon will be – the parents of our Golden Age children. Now, these pure, shimmering, loving, little ones-of-Light are descending to Earth, in great numbers, with peace and Divine Love in their hearts. Nothing can prevent their arrival.

They are arriving into the homes of parents who are pure and loving inhabitants of Earth in this new age of enlightenment and who have no need of worn-out rules and regulations, or of dogma and doctrines belonging to a bygone era. They are intelligent, educated, caring and loving people who are open to new ideas and new concepts, as well as being in touch with their own inner guidance and their *feeling* nature. As such, they are free to pursue their own unique pathways to spiritual enlightenment and advancement, untrammelled by old, decrepit concepts and without interference from others who are steeped in questionable philosophies that were altered by others in times long past. The parents of the golden ones will guide the new arrivals wisely.

Disturbingly, ones who are vibrating at a frequency consistent with that of the two lower chakras *only*, may feel a hand placed on their shoulder at the conclusion of this lifetime and they may hear the dreaded words that they believed would never be heard by them. These words are: *It is time.*

The Discourses in this book elaborate further on this matter. For those ones, the Akashic Records may be opened and all of their former lifetimes will be exposed. Then, they will know that their own life-experiences on the plane-of-Earth are at an end. Assuming that what these Discourses state has a ring of truth to it, there is no time left for them to redress the terrible deeds that they have orchestrated, or that they have allowed to occur in lifetimes past. The previous practice of the wealthy being able to purchase plenary indulgences on their death-beds will be seen as the futile exercise that it is – and has been always. How could such a purchase secure a place for them *in heaven* anyway? What a preposterous idea that was.

As for the children-of-Light, in their daily prayers and meditations, they will find all of their own answers and their own direction in this, their present life-experience.

Returning once more to the scenario that was described earlier, in the meditation exercise in **ERA of DISCERNMENT,** let us explore this matter a little further, with regard to gathering in groups for the purpose of meditation and, most especially, with the intent of aiding the planet as she attempts to heal herself.

If all of the participants in these groups who were meeting in spiritual circles, were to link into Mother Earth's vibration in this manner, thereby raising their own vibratory frequency to an extremely high degree (through Divine Love and Divine Light), this would be a wonderful experience for all. At the same time, they could link (at the etheric/Astral level) with others of like-mind and of pure, loving intent who were situated elsewhere on this planet, so as to create a massive and an awesome effect everywhere.

If this phenomenon were to spread then, as a gigantic wave of Love Energy and Love Essence, to encompass the entire planet and to become a planetary experience – as has occurred with the annual Earth Hour when electrically-generated lights are extinguished voluntarily and temporarily – the result may be that we have this planet changing from a third-dimensional one almost overnight.

Earth may become, once again, the fourth-dimensional, brilliant Creation of God – just as she was in the beginning. In this case, Mother Earth would have returned to her original and most beautiful state.

What a magnificent spectacle that would be for all of us to behold!

Stella McMillan Series

So, there is one other question to be asked. For whom was the *Stella McMillan* Series written?

First and foremost, these books were written, in the form of two trilogies, to be enjoyed by the parents, grandparents, caregivers and guardians of the new babies who are arriving in great numbers now. These new little beings are floating down to Earth (via the birth experience) and they are flooding this dark planet with their Love Energy and Essence.

But, who is there to teach and to guide these little ones who are soft, gentle, kind and loving, as well as being wide open to new experiences? Is it the ones who preach the dogma and doctrines of a bygone era that were recorded long, long ago and which were intended for ones who were not as enlightened as those who are residing on Earth today? And, was it a fact that the population of that time was unenlightened, simply because those ones who were the self-appointed rulers and counsellors wished it to be so?

It is for others to decide on the answers to these questions. For my part, I will reinforce simply the thoughts of Louisa Lyndhurst, within the pages of Book Two of the Series. In **ERROR PERPETUATED**, Louisa declared forcefully to Charles that no one could prevent a mother from instructing her child. How true that statement is!

As explained more fully in these Discourses, our Golden Age babies – wide-eyed with wonder and awe – are coming to us in great numbers now. And, truly, we are blessed!

We cannot afford to allow anyone to *mis*-lead and to *mis*-guide them. Remember the manner, in which young James Lyndhurst and his sister, Mary, were subjected to persistent and systematic conditioning throughout their young lives by their mother's uncle/priest in the Victorian story.

It would not be wise to allow a similar situation to arise with our Golden Age babes. They are too precious and too innocent to be treated in a terrible manner such as that. As the Discourses reveal, they are dropping down, as gentle, clear, clean and long-awaited raindrops do, to the lower vibration of Earth, from a great height and from a place where negativity does not exist. They will need to be nurtured and guided by ones who have at least a basic understanding of the tenets of the Golden Age of Enlightenment, which has commenced.

Presumably, we will be able to recognise them easily. They will be incapable of hiding their brilliance. With all of these little ones, they will have Divine Love and Divine Light streaming unceasingly from their bright, bright eyes!

In order to teach, guard and guide these beautiful and blessed Golden Age babies, it is the parents, grandparents, caregivers and guardians who will need to take over this responsibility. The age-old, tired, tried and supposedly-true way is dead, because it has become stymied and it has lost the Energy and Essence of Divine Love – this being Universal, Unconditional Love.

There is no other way. So, please, open the mind wide – and the heart even wider still.

Step bravely forward into the Age of Aquarius with the knowledge and the confidence that every step will be guided from within one's own being. After all, is not the man, who is carrying the water-pitcher walking across our skies now? And is not the sign of Aquarius exactly that symbol?

Most definitely, the time has come for all thoughtful, caring and loving **Piscean children-of-Light** to become the soft, gentle, kind and loving **Aquarian adolescents-of-Light,** while being steeped in Divine Wisdom.

Stella McMillan
25 October, 2012

Epilogue

With mid-December of 2012 came a horror that few could contemplate. Twenty sweet, little angles-of-Light left the planet together. Earth became a much darker place with their passing from physical life. These angels, along with their extraordinary teachers, showed the world the meaning of a sacrifice for the good of the whole.

If one were to look *through physical eyes only*, one would see carnage on an unimaginable scale. No doubt the ones who were first on the scene of the horrendous, senseless massacre of innocent, young children thought so. Those images will be with them for the remainder of their lives.

With the perpetrator, one would see an angry and demented creature who would evoke little understanding and sympathetic feelings from a shocked and outraged community.

To look *through the eyes of Spirit*, a slightly different picture would emerge. The attacker would have been someone who, by his own free will and over a period of many lifetimes, had closed down all of his chakras one-by-one to the point where only his Base point would be open. This would allow him to function at a physical level, but not participate. In such a state, he would feel powerless, with even his Sacral chakra, the point of Divine Power, closed. He would believe himself to be *powerless* unless and until he had a weapon of mass destruction in his hands.

Whether the weapon is a military machine or an aircraft to fly into a building where thousands of people are gathered, it matters not. The innocent pay the price always when ones such as these become angry and frustrated. Rarely will they acknowledge that the systematic closing of their chakras, over a long period of time, has brought about a tragic outcome.

To peer *through the eyes of Spirit* at the twenty little angels-of-Light who had brought their great Love and Light to a darkened world, another picture emerges. Their arrival en masse on the planet within the previous seven years was a case of the Illumined Ones descending in order to spread the Light and Love of God. They chose a certain small town. They chose to come as a group of angels into physical form. Their angelic teachers were their shepherds. Some survived. Some did not.

That small town of a few thousand people would have been shining like the brightest beacon imaginable with their arrival. It was a town whose Light was so bright that someone who was in dense negativity had but two choices. Leave and walk away from the Light; or, do all in his power to dim the Light of God. He chose attack unfortunately and these beautiful Golden Ones have returned now to the realms of Spirit to be comforted in the arms of the angels who love them dearly.

Arming the teachers with weapons would not have prevented the carnage. This was a case of the Light and Love of God being focussed in one, particular place and at one specific period of Earth time. How many more of our newly-arrived Illumined Ones will meet a similar fate in the years to come? The answer to this question will depend entirely on the manner, in which humanity deals with the darkness within its midst. That darkness is positioned in every community and in every country. Prayer is the answer. Love is the key.

The Final Thread?

As mentioned in the *Prologue*, world events do have a habit of intervening to alter the pre-planned life-paths of many who incarnate on Earth.

For example, looking back at recent history, the event that was most likely the trigger for the commencement of World War One was the callous, pre-meditated assassination of the Archduke Ferdinand of Austria on 28 June, 1914. Exactly one month later, war commenced between Austria and Serbia. Then, on 4 August, 1914, it spread to encompass most of Europe, with the exception of Italy, at that stage. This horrific conflict, known as the *war-to-end-all-wars*, continued until 1918. Presumably, many would have left their physical bodies well ahead of their appointed time.

After this war, the event that was seen as the trigger for the start of the next horrific war, known as World War Two, happened. This was the invasion of Poland in September, 1939.

Between the conclusion of the First World War and the commencement of the Second World War, there was a period of peace. That peace lasted for twenty-one years. This was sufficient time for another generation of beautiful beings to be born and to grow to maturity on a dark planet. Consequently, many more innocent people would have abandoned physical life – and, prematurely, one would assume – during the horrendous period of the Second World War.

Between the ending of world-wide hostilities in 1945 and the occurrence of the catastrophic nuclear explosions at Chernobyl, in Ukraine, in April, 1986, another forty-one years elapsed. During that time-frame, there were wars occurring on the planet, in Vietnam and Lebanon to name but two.

In one language of Earth, Chernobyl means *black forest*. In another language, black forest means *Wormwood*.

Was the arrival of Halley's Comet, in February, 1986, a sign to herald that which was to come? By April of that same year, a toxic and deadly cloud, with long-term cancerous effects, began to drift over parts of western and northern Europe. It brought death and devastation in its wake as it spread out – as an open fan does – from its source at Chernobyl. Many more people would have departed this life prematurely, due to this continuing catastrophe.

In 1990/91 and following on from the Chernobyl tragedy, there was a war that lasted for five months. This terrible war began near to the River Euphrates in Iraq.

How many more innocent people lost their lives as a result of that next man-made disaster? Were these events all foretold of in prophecy at an earlier period of Earth's history?

Then, almost a decade later and in late September of 2000, three prominent world leaders parted company after many days of deliberations. Two of them returned to their respective countries. Publicly, they announced that no agreement could be reached to resolve the great differences between their countries. It was rumoured widely that secret negotiations continued between two of these men in Israel and that an historic agreement was reached. However, before this agreement could be announced to the world, a military man and leader-of-men took matters into his own hands. He led an entourage to the most sacred of sites where his enemies worshipped. Outrage followed this very public event and the Second Intifada was born.

One year, one week and one day later, coalition troops invaded Afghanistan and another devastating and bloody war was underway. Raging in tandem with the war in Afghanistan was the second Gulf War, which was being waged in Iraq.

How was it that these events could have been predicted almost two thousand years earlier? There is but one prophecy yet to eventuate. It is so frightening a prospect that it does not bear contemplation. However, the Mother – this being Earth – may have a hand to play yet, before this predicted catastrophe comes to pass while being orchestrated by ones who are incarnate on her surface presently. Time will tell on that score.

There was one other scenario that came into play, also, during those years between 1914 and the present time of 2013. That event was the discovery of a comet, which had the planet of Jupiter in its path. The comet was named Shoemaker-Levy, after the team who discovered it on March 24, 1994. It crashed into Jupiter in July of that year while the population of Earth watched in awe from afar.

If the one known as J'shua bar Joseph, who became known as Jesus, The Christ, was born in 6 BC – as seems to be the widely-accepted year of his birth (due to an acknowledged miscalculation when a certain calendar was being recorded) – the 1994 comet crashed into Jupiter exactly two thousand years after his birth. Was this event a coincidence or a case of perfect timing as a warning to a warring humanity to lay aside its weapons and to embrace peace?

Of course, this has not occurred and the streets where he walked two thousand years ago – preaching Peace on Earth and Goodwill to All – are bathed in blood now. There appears to be little hope of stemming the flow, or of stopping the carnage that continues unabated there.

Not only are these events, occurring between 1914 and 2013, a reason to pause for thought, but also they are a stark reminder of *man's inhumanity to man* in acts that are barbaric and unloving in the extreme.

At this time, are we but months away not only from the first one-hundred year anniversary of Archduke Ferdinand's assassination, but also possibly the same anniversary of the start of the prophecies of Revelation? And, are the *two witnesses* due to make their appearance?

Perhaps, the well-publicised prophecies of Nostradamus and the visions of the Irish Catholic bishop, St. Malachy – when viewed in conjunction with the Revelation prophecies – may be seen to dovetail into one another. The astute reader may see that, of the future popes of the Church of Rome that St. Malachy described in his visions of 1140 AD, one hundred and eleven have appeared, with Pope Benedict XVI being the second last one. According to those prophetic visions, the last pope will be required to leave Rome early in his reign, due to a catastrophic occurrence. Will the new pope of 2013 be the last pope to reside in Rome on a permanent basis?

More details on these visions appear in the book, 'THE LAST POPE – The Decline and Fall of the Church of Rome – *The Prophecies of St. Malachy for the New Millennium*' by the author, John Hogue.

Almost one century of Earth's time has elapsed since the commencement of hostilities that possibly marked the beginning of those prophecies. Most have passed by and are events consigned to history now. There is only the last *big one* to be completed. So, will the last one be played out to its final conclusion? Will there be Divine Intervention to end the suffering of the once-beautiful Mother – this being Earth?

It is stated in these Discourses that Earth is convulsing now. Her tremors are terrible to watch, for those with *eyes that can see*. Her storms are ferocious. Her frozen wastelands are melting at an alarming rate. Once these tremors and the storms have moved through her Being, while being her fear and her anger on display for all to witness, her wastelands melt. Are these really her tears of terror and distress on display?

Many people can see and understand what is occurring, but they do not know how to help her. Unfortunately, all that some humans can see are the advantages for them individually as they study the minerals beneath her surface, on which they walk. Most look upon all of these happenings with the eyes of the physical body. Only when an awakened humanity peers with *the eyes of the spirit-self* can the true situation be revealed and understood fully.

Many forward-thinking people do so now and they are in horror and despair as they realise the full implications of what is occurring on Earth. They feel powerless to stop the ones who control everyone and everything on the planet. It appears that these ones vibrate at the level of the Sacral chakra of Divine Power. They are motivated by greed and the strong desire to control others while they are never seen to be involved personally. They are never in the direct firing-line. They are devoid of all feelings. They are devoid of Love Unconditional and compassion. They believe that they are untouchable. They believe that they will never be called to account for their terrible deeds. The Discourses, when encapsulated, state this clearly.

God has their measure. They do not believe in God.

God will have the last word as God had the First Word.

God will bring life on Earth to a standstill.

All will stand in wonder, in awe and in fear when this moment arrives. Does this event need to occur? These writings state, also, that this is a very serious question for humanity to contemplate. But, will anyone take the time to do so? It is stressed that there is time still to pull back – for some, that is. For others, the die is cast. By their own volition, in successive lifetimes, they have chosen freely to walk the *power*-path to self-destruction. For some others, it would seem that a period of Grace is available. Turn to God now. Ask for assistance. Ask for guidance. Ask to be shown The Way. This seems to be the overriding message contained there, within these writings.

However, others may interpret these Discourses differently. Probably, most will either ridicule or ignore them. Where will the madness and mayhem end? That is a question, with which humanity will need to grapple in the years ahead. Will there need to be Divine Intervention, as the Discourses appear to suggest, in order for the planet to be saved from the destructive forces that seek to destroy her completely? Or, will humanity – as a whole – stand up and say: "enough is enough"? The answer hangs in the balance, it would seem.

As the Discourses stress, humanity collectively has destroyed this once-beautiful planet. No one can deny this statement. Animals, as a species, are electing to leave permanently, due to the excessive cruelty that has been metered out to their particular species by those who are considered to be more intelligent. Often, one must pause to wonder.

Where indeed will it end? The whole sorry scenario will need to be brought to an end by Divine Intervention once again. If these writings have been recorded correctly, this has happened before, it would appear, when humanity reached this stage of development and brought the planet to the brink. Water was the cleanser back then, in the Age of Leo, when pride was to the fore, although which Age of Leo is not stated.

Afterwards, life began again on a pristine planet. Have the lessons of Leo been learned by the population who inhabits Earth currently? The Discourse included in this book and entitled *The Rose* might give a clue to one possible scenario. Was this what occurred during the final moments – mid-way through the Age of Leo – by the ones who were *awake* and *aware*? Did the sleepy-ones succumb to the great flood? Did the wise ones ask God for help and for guidance back then? Must we take the time now to listen-within for guidance once assistance is sought? And, must we be prepared to go against the tide of public opinion and perhaps to accept public censure once that guidance is acted upon, at a personal level? This task is the most difficult one of all, especially when cynical ones question our every move and every motive.

Carrying through with the necessary physical action will be difficult. Was it this way for the ones who worked tirelessly to build their seafaring vessels prior to the great flood occurring? Was 'The Ark' of history simply an analogy? It was stated in the Discourses that many such vessels were built by brave, forward-thinking souls and many, many thousands were saved. Then, life began again on a refreshed planet. Did it begin again on the different mountain-tops of Earth and on places that were above the level of the flood? Was the story of the great flood written into the folklore of all surviving groups for future generations to know and to understand? The messages that appear to be contained within these writings are these: pull back from the brink now, before it is too late. This can be achieved only through Divine Love and through asking for help from the Source-of-ALL-Love-and-Light. Ask and you shall receive always. Time is short now.

However, others may come to another conclusion, through the reading of the seventeen Discourses. God's Law can be flouted for only so long. Then, the piper must be paid. Is that the lesson of Leo? Did the destruction of Earth's second moon cause the disaster? This was a theory that was circulating for decades within New Age groups at the end of the twentieth century. What will be the trigger next time? Will the loving ones who are incarnate on Earth now allow a next time?

That is for humanity collectively to answer, but time is of the essence. According to the Discourses, a silent army of Light Workers needs to rise up in prayer while asking for relief and for a way to be shown. Pray and meditate daily. Listen within. All will be revealed to the attentive heart. Planet Earth will bless all who intervene on her behalf. She is such a gentle soul. Appease her anger. Ease her fears. Dry her tears of despair. Give her hope so that her sun can shine brightly again and her one and only moon can glow with the brilliance of two moons as she mourns her missing sister.

God is the answer. Faith is the key. Prayer is the method. Love will rule all, for all eternity.

Stella McMillan
28 June, 2013.

Gerard's Last Message

Pre-set Pathways

In every lifetime, two pathways are pre-set. The spiritual road is the all-important one for the incoming soul-spirit who is embarking on an exciting adventure in the lower realm of the physical world.

The other blueprint is the physical road map. Its purpose is to give physical support in an emotional and a financial sense for the most part. One is the real pathway. The other road – this being the physical one – is the support system.

Rarely does this come to fruition once the physical life begins in earnest. By the second phase of life, at approximately fourteen years of age, the die is cast usually. By this stage, the spiritual aspect of life has receded almost totally while the consciousness is focussed fully on physical pursuits and pleasures. At this point, the ego-self is in complete control. The spirit-self has taken a back seat, being but the passive observer. All of the plans, hopes and dreams of a spiritual nature have been abandoned and are left for a future embodiment.

Sometimes, due to hardship and difficulties experienced in the physical world, the spirit-self may be handed control temporarily. But, for the most part, the ego-self resumes control once the difficulties in life have been surmounted.

When one returns to the Astral plane after every life experience, the usual reaction is: "Oh! No, not again!"

Once the ego-personality self is defeated while in physical embodiment on Earth and the spirit-self takes charge completely, the spiritual life of the individual concerned is all that there is. This is a voluntary relinquishing of power by the ego-self.

It is then that the physical life and the Astral life merge As-One. The garden of Light and Love is all that there is, for the New Jerusalem has become the only reality for the one in embodiment on Earth.

Truly then, the wonder of life is revealed through this magnificent resurrection!

Consciousness

Those of a *limited consciousness* have chosen freely to live inside the leaning tower. There, they vibrate at the frequency of the third dimension.

Those of an *expanded consciousness* have chosen freely to reside on the temporary verandah. There, they vibrate at a frequency that is midway between the third and fourth dimensions.

Those of an *enlightened consciousness* have chosen freely to reside, for the most part, in the garden of Light and Love – that being Divine Light and Divine Love. They choose to visit the verandah infrequently and only when they determine that those visits are necessary for the good-of-the-whole. The garden is a fourth dimensional reality.

The majority of the population of the lower garden lives on the verandah. The verandah is being demolished rapidly. When it exists no longer, the tower will fall. So, it is the verandah-dwellers who need to choose where they will reside in the future.

Those of a limited consciousness, as with those of an enlightened consciousness, have chosen already their future and their destiny. This was a free-will choice on the part of all.

The games of the third dimensional garden are at an end.
Peace be with you. *Adieu.*

Lamb of Love

The poem, **Lamb of Love**, which is included here, was written on 30
September, 2012, during the day of the full moon of that month. Its
meaning is veiled where timing is concerned. This could be referring
to conception, to birth, or it could be a reference to a Second Coming.
The interpretation is left to the reader.

Other Poems

The poem, ***Eternal Call,*** appears on my website, as well as in an
earlier book of this Series. This poem is repeated here for the consider-
ation of those who wish to review it, along with its poignant message.

Similarly, the poem, **The Veil**, which appeared in the Book,
ERROR of UNDERSTANDING, is included here, at the conclu-
sion of this book, as is ***DIVINE JADE*** from the sixth book of the
Stella McMillan *Series.*

Other Discourses and Publications

There are other Discourses that I have written in recent times.
However, there were too many to be recorded in this small book. As
well, several books were published previously in the *Stella McMillan*
Series and these were mainly spiritual writings, although some may
consider them to be pure fiction. These titles are listed at the conclusion of this book.

For those who are interested in reading those earlier writings that
contain information pertinent only to ones who are seeking spiritual
solutions to complex questions, I will release these earlier books and
the new Discourses shortly. Full details will appear on my website for
those who are interested.

www.stellamcmillan.com.au

Lamb of Love

The Dove of Peace descends this day.
The Lamb of Love comes to the fray.
The turmoil of Earth continues to play.
In a land far-away, his head he did lay.

Far, far from turmoil of earthly care,
far, far from fear of earthly war,
in a place of beauty, free from fear,
the Great Southern Land protects him there.

His blanket is one of protection from harm.
His parents the Light of all who come
to see, to know, to follow, to form
the nucleus of a family formed in Love.

Divine Light, Divine Wisdom, Divine Will
are hallmark signs of this child of Love.
Divine Love is his only signature still.
With Balance, Power and Life, he is above.

Above all, above Earth, above turmoil, strife –
guile unknown, he offers hope in life.
The Lamb of Love comes to still the flame,
to lighten the load, to heal – not enflame.

To enflame with a passion for God Everlasting
to a world torn apart, hatred rising,
He comes in Love, in Peace, in Blessed Joy.
Welcome him all, our precious, golden boy!

Stella McMillan
30 September, 2012

Stella McMillan Series

In Conclusion

I have lived before this body.
I have lived within this body.
I have lived in other realities beyond Earth.
I will live long after this body has disintegrated.
I will live long after this body is dust and ashes.

To this end, I carry on with my physical life in the full knowledge
that I AM more than this body of physical flesh.

I AM more than flesh, blood and bone.
I AM more than the conscious mind of this body.
I AM immortal and eternal.
I AM a visitor to this planet at present.
I live in this world, but I AM not of it.

Thus is the true meaning of Resurrection revealed.

In God, I AM safe.
In God, I AM loved.
In God, I AM secure.
In God, I AM pure Light as I AM pure Love.

God is my ALL!

Stella McMillan
15 November, 2012

The Veil

To "know" the meaning of Life
is to lift the veil of Death.
To lift the etheric film beyond Life
is to peer into the mist beyond Time.
Through the mist is revealed Reality.
In this Realm, ALL ways are seen

To peer into another Reality
is to look both ways – ALL ways.
To peer forward beyond the NOW
is to look into the Future.
To search backwards before the NOW
is to look into the mist before Time!

To "know" True Reality
is to look every which way.
For that which has gone before
and that which is to go beyond
is all the same – the ONE,
a part of the ALL – Super-Consciousness!

Stella McMillan
5 May, 2007

Eternal Call

A diamond of great rarity fell to Earth.
It was pure; it was clear; it was superb.
Dust covered its purity as its journey began.
Whispering winds rolled it along in the sand.
Sands of time cracked its pristine surface a little.
As mud filled its cracks, sun made it brittle.
A Hand lifted it high; its Creator's Breath soothed.
Rest and refuge was its harbour beneath the moon.
Again, this diamond fell on Earth's surface,
though no longer so pure, nor so clear, but still superb
beneath the collection of dust, sand, mud of Earth!

In all its lifetimes since before time began,
the Heart of the diamond pulsed beneath sand,
mud, dust, grit and grime – alive at its Heart.
In time with the Creator's Beat, it was never apart.
Light, Love, Wisdom, Will, Order, Power, Life Divine
were the Hallmark Traits of this diamond sublime.
Difficult to recognise by a glance at its surface;
there was little to recommend it to ones of taste.
Others saw only its outer shell – not its Core.
Illusion reigned supreme. Unrecognisable, though pure –
still pure – a diamond of great beauty roamed on Earth!

Eternal Call

Its covering was its protection against pain.
No matter the trials of rock, wind, sun and rain,
at its Heart, it pulsed still to its Creator's Sound.
To 'OHMN-of-Life', its soul continued to pound.
Many, many times, it returned – at its Creator's Call –
to Nirvana to recharge, regenerate after its fall.
In all diamond's excursions, its covering grew more dense.
In all diamond's travels, the journey made less sense.
Until diamond discovered the truth of the trek
was to come to the understanding of its hidden depth.
At its Core Centre, it was a diamond of great rarity!

As a rolling stone gathers no moss, diamond's need
was to rid itself of sand, mud, grime and to heal.
To all Earth's physicians did diamond appeal.
But, none could help, for they, too, must heal.
'Physician, heal thyself,' became the catch-cry.
All sought a way to redeem and to try
to return to their original seed – the diamond sublime.
Some had shut off Divine Light; others Love Divine;
Divine Wisdom, Divine Will, many denied.
With Divine Order out-of-balance, Life
was left to partner Power – Creator's Tune lost!

Eternal Call

As every diamond on Earth's surface grew more dense,
The Mother suffered pain, loss, degradation immense.
Her heart heavy, she sank to despair. Her desperation
caused a response that shook every vibration
within her Being and every diamond upon her surface.
Fear reigned. Panic followed. Despair on every face.
Nation fought nation. At every Age, the Diamond Master –
Amilus, Enoch, Melchizedek, Pythagoras, Gautama,
Zoroaster of Persia –appeared to lead the Race.
In many forms, to many nations, He came –
this Diamond of Light Divine; Love Unmeasured.

ᘒᕒ

He was glorified, deified, crucified, vilified.
He forgave; then, came again and again to Earth's tribe.
As Jew, as Greek, as Indian, as Persian and more
to lead by example, to heal, to teach the LAW.
The LAW-of-ONE was his theme; his simple way
misunderstood; his simple life too difficult a way.
The tribe rebelled – broke away. Planet's diamonds lost.
Aquarius brought point-of-no-return. Ignored by most,
water-carrier, with pitcher held high and aloft,
Piscean Christ's lessons forgotten or scoffed.
Hope for diamond's return all but lost!

Eternal Call

"Where to from here?" Many asked in vain.
Return to the Creator to be healed of pain.
Illusion's way not the answer diamond sought.
Diamond's Heart pulsed, but time was so short.
Unseen, unheard, Creator called and called.
The Master's Voice was that of Maitreya, the Lord.
He came in many guises. All awaited His next birth.
Shoemaker-Levy was 'shot-across-bow' of Earth.
Next comes 'the rock' so large, so close, so fiery.
Will it shave by, within a whisker, is query.
Or, hit with a shudder, scattering diamonds a-plenty?

Earth 'on the move, ready-or-not', Creator does cry.
Diamonds run hither-and-thither; nowhere to hide.
Creator's Love Song continues; unheard by most.
'OHMN' is the sound wave; 'LOVE' all but lost.
Planet shudders and shakes; fire out-of-control.
Rock demolishes satellites; oceans roar; waves roll.
Never has the like been witnessed before.
Even Noah, in Age of Leo – after Atlantis did fall,
could envisage a disaster to equal Earth's upheaval.
Second Woe is all over in one, swift reversal –
all over in 'no-time'. Survivors ponder the cause!

Eternal Call

Cause-and-Effect is answer, of course; Cosmic Law
overrides law of king, prince, pope, priest and ALL.
Diamond's called HOME – "Come, one and all!"
Time for tea-party; time for reflection/overhaul.
Life is ongoing for our diamonds on journey
as they trek from one life to another endlessly.
Lack of understanding, at spiritual level, the cause;
Time for tea and rejuvenation; ALL must now pause.
Pathway is winding; Life never-ending in reality.
True Reality beckons; Akashic Books open to scrutiny.
Karmic debt accounted as ledger displayed!

Planet now cleansed – not healed at core.
Return requested – most diamonds implore.
Request denied for many with unpaid score.
Lesson of Unconditional Love most did ignore.
Sorrow great; wailing, wishing greater still
as many ponder the reason, ignoring Divine Will.
Divine Light brought Illumination, but centre locked.
Divine Wisdom, Divine Will, Divine Love blocked.
Divine Order out-of-balance for most still;
Divine Power, Divine Life flout Divine Will.
"Piper to be paid" brought life to a stand-still!

Eternal Call

"How can this be?" became catch-cry of ALL.
Creator's Song unheard – on deaf ears 'OHMN' did fall.
Uncomprehending, diamonds request immediate return.
Love's Lesson unlearned. The Mother badly burned.
Cause-and-Effect misunderstood by most souls.
Rejuvenated planet needs to heal and console.
Children's destruction too horrific to describe;
pollution, degradation, money ruled tribe.
Only Pure Diamonds trusted with Earth's care.
All others a thousand years watch from afar.
Wail, weep, while Creator unmoved; Song unheard!

Clear all dust, sand, mud, grit and grime.
Start at outer level, one layer at a time.
Only answer is this – to heal oneself now.
Only then can 'Eternal OHMN' be re-found.
Only then can God's children hear The Sound
of Creator's Song once again; once more re-bound.
Diamonds of great rarity fall to Earth again,
when ALL is pure! ALL clear! ALL superb then!
Mother Earth hears the 'OHMN Sound' clearly.
Why, then, cannot all be attuned really?
Diamonds listen! Diamonds hear! Divine Light awaits!

Stella McMillan
(during blue moon time-frame on 1ˢᵗ January, 2010).

Who is she?

There is a Secret and Sacred Truth.

All must seek her alone.

Sealed lips only must speak her name.

Who is this precious gem?

She is:

"Divine Jade"

Divine Jade

In a moment of Truth, Violet Flame awakens.

Sight is revealed in a flicker.

Ruby Red awakens.

Cord lengthens as Touch is revealed.

Yellow-Gold flickers awake.

Fragrance is the prize as blossoms breathe
out their sweet aroma come fresh from the

Breath of God.

Blue Soul arises.

The call of the dove is heard.

Memory stirs as, Vital and Radiant,

The Spirit emerges.

The Divinity of Royal Jade

more Radiant than one thousand suns

of Earth – is revered.

No power can hold her. She is –

Divine Jade

BOOKS – THE GOLDEN AGE and FAMILY OF MAN

These two, small books were written and published in Australia by Beverly Bree in 1991/1992. Excerpts follow here. Some copies of these books are available. Details will appear on my website: **www.stellamcmillan.com.au**

THE GOLDEN AGE
There can be no thoughts greater
than those directed towards God.

SPIRITUAL PATH

Every time I incarnate, I arrive knowing
I am here to follow a pre-determined path.
Assuming I remain on my spiritual path,
I am doing God's Will, not mine.
Therefore, when I depart,
the world is a better place for my having been here.
If everyone were to follow intuition,
which is blessed by the energy of God, then the world would be
as God intended – a wonderful place to live!

CHILDREN OF LIGHT

All life's problems stem from fear and indecision.
Fear and indecision stem from doubt.
Doubt is caused by negativity.
Negativity is walking in the shadows,
away from God's Light.
To walk in God's Light, we must become Children of Light, for
only Children of Light will be selected to enter
the Golden Age.
The selection process has begun.

THE SELECTION PROCESS

To be eligible for selection, we must become DETACHED from all of life's ATTACHMENTS, such as people, possessions and pleasures.

We must submit willingly to this cleansing process
so that the dross may be burnt away from self
and we become as crystal,
clearly and brightly reflecting
God's Light and Love from all angles,
walking through life in a detached manner, as Jesus did, being
non-judgemental and non-discriminatory,
loving all for God's sake and for no other reason.
Humility is the key.
To be successful, the candidate must pass all tests along God's spiritual path.

LOVE AND CHOICE

The opposite of fear and indecision is love and choice.
Children of Light must choose:
- love over fear,
- peace over war,
- positivity over negativity,
- intuition over logical thought,
- soul over Self,
- feelings over emotion,
- spirituality over personality,
- harmony over disharmony,
- happiness over sadness,
- light over dark,
- God above all else.

The road is clear; walk only in the light,
for that light is the Divine Light of God
that shines from within us all.
The Children of Light will be shining
so brightly in the Golden Age that they will be as beacons for all
to see and to follow.
So come, Child of Light, dispel all doubt.
Tread the path of Light in faith and humility.

LOVE AND WAR

War is caused by fear.
It is not so much a fear of others
as it is a fear of themselves.
People who fear do not trust in themselves and consequently,
they do not trust in anything anymore. Why?
Because they have ceased trusting in God.

They no longer trust in God,
for they no longer believe in God.
They have stopped believing in God,
placing all their belief and trust in Self.
But Self is plagued by doubt.
Fear and indecision begin to creep
through the tiny chink in Self's armour.
Self-esteem is the first casualty;
self-love is the second.
Negativity takes a hold of the soul
and the soul walks in darkness,
away from the Divine Light of God.
War will not cease until humankind learns
to trust and to love unconditionally.

LOVE AND TRUST

Love and trust in God first.
Listen within and love and trust
that small, all-knowing voice of Spirit,
for that is the direction from
God within one's self.
Follow that direction without question;
then, and only then, will one be able
to love those who one does not trust,
making peace with them
while living and trusting in the
Light and Love of God.
Love will cast out fear,
which is the root of all war.
War will cease on Planet Earth.

SPIRIT WITHIN

The voice within comes from Spirit.
Spirit is soft,
Spirit is gentle, kind and loving.
Any thought, word or deed that is not
soft, gentle, kind and loving
does not come from Spirit
but from the personality, which is Self.
Spirit is the Divine Light and Love of God.
Deny Self and live by Spirit
and truly will you become a beacon
    -    A Child of Light,
an integral part of the Golden Age.

PERFECT BALANCE

God is perfect balance.
God is perfect love.
In order to have balance in our lives,
we must juggle constantly between
spiritual wisdom and practical solutions,
between physical insights and spiritual solutions.

Fear and indecision are signs of Self love.
To live in God's perfect love,
we must follow His Will
and then we will have
perfect balance in our lives.

HUMILITY

Humility is the key to faith.
Faith cannot be separated from humility.
When true humility and deep faith
possess the soul, Self disappears,
submerged in God Whose wisdom,
power, magnificence and eternal
greatness have become as one,
thus the glory of the Kingdom
of God is truly found.

Bibliography

Book Titles mentioned in this book:
Hands of Light
Light Emerging
Author: Barbara Ann Brennan
Publisher: Bantam Books, New York, USA
The Creation of Health
Authors: C. Norman Shealy M. D. Ph. D
               Caroline M. Myss M.A.
Publisher: Stillpoint Publishing, New Hampshire, USA
THE HOLY BLOOD AND THE HOLY GRAIL
Authors: Michael Baigent, Richard Leigh & Henry Lincoln
Publisher: The Random House Group Limited, London
Peter, Paul & Mary Magdalene
THE FOLLOWERS OF JESUS IN HISTORY AND LEGEND
Author: Bart D. Ehrman
Publisher: Oxford University Press Inc. New York
THE LAST POPE – The Decline and Fall of the Church of
Rome – The Prophecies of St. Malachy for the New
Millennium
Author: John Hogue
Publisher: Element Books Limited, UK
The Secret Supper **A Novel**
Author: Javier Sierra – Translator – Alberto Manguel
Publisher: SIMON & SCHUSTER UK

Other:

Lyrics/song: **I'D LIVE MY LIFE OVER WITH YOU**
Daniel O'Donnell – Brockwell/Demon Music

Movie/film: *AVATAR*
A James Cameron Film Twentieth Century Fox

Stella McMillan Series

To access the *Stella McMillan* website:
www.stellamcmillan.com.au

Books/eBooks by *Stella McMillan*

First Trilogy: *ERA/ERROR of UNDERSTANDING*
Book One   *ERROR of UNDERSTANDING*
Book Two   *ERROR PERPETUATED*
Book Three   *ERA of UNDERSTANDING*

Second Trilogy: *ERA/ERROR of DISCERNMENT*
Book One   *AWAKENING TO AWARENESS*
Book Two   *ERROR PROFOUND*
Book Three   *ERA of DISCERNMENT*

Companion Book to *Stella McMillan* Trilogies:
SUSPENSION – Between Two Realms –

Earlier Books by *Stella McMillan*:
UNDERCOVER STARSEEDS – Published 2000
THE REAL BOOK, REAL BEGINNING
Published 1999
The Tenets of the Law-of-One – Published 2002

Books by Beverly Bree
THE GOLDEN AGE (ISBN 0 646 11179 8)
FAMILY OF MAN (ISBN 0 646 11800 8)
Published 1992 – National Library of Australia, Canberra.